PRA
JAIM
JME BOOKS

l. Ron Hubbard Writers of the Future Award
BRAG Medallion Honoree Award
Top Ten Book of 2014 Kid Lit Reviews

"…the world Engle has created in this novel is an intriguing one, equal parts familiar and fantastic." *Kirkus Reviews*

"…belongs on your bookshelf - young or old - right along with Tolkien and Grimm." –Amazon.com

"I did not want to leave until the last page was turned." –Kid Lit Reviews

"…the same kind of universe you might meet Captain Malcolm Reynolds or Luke Skywalker in." –The Story Sanctuary Reviews

"Jaimie Engle brings "The Dredge" to an exciting, unexpected, and ultimately satisfying ending." –Third Flatiron Editor

Cutting-Edge Storytelling
www.jmebooks.com

BOOKS BY JAIMIE ENGLE

FICTION

Clifton Chase and the Arrow of Light
A boy is chosen to change the past by a magic arrow

Clifton Chase and the Arrow of Light:
the Coloring Book
Condensed version of the novel with pictures to color

The Dredge
Supernatural gifts are sought through deception in a future world

Dreadlands: Wolf Moon
A Viking boy must face shifting wolves or become their prey

NON-FICTION

Writing Your Novel, using the Bible as your guide (book 1)
Learn how to write your book by studying the book of Genesis

Visit the author at thewriteengle.com.

the *Write* engle

THE
TOILET
PAPERS

places to go while you go

Jaimie Engle

JME Books

Published in the United States by JME Books,
a division of A Writer For Life, LLC,
Melbourne, FL 32935.

Visit us on the Web: thewriteengle.com

For an author visit or bulk order discounts, visit us at
thewriteengle.com or email thewriteengle@gmail.com.

Summary: A collection of short stories to make your bathroom break a
pleasure.

ISBN-10: 0-9971709-8-0
ISBN-13: 978-0-9971709-8-6

10 9 8 7 6 5 4 3 2

Cutting-Edge Storytelling with a Supernatural Slant
JME Books

This book is dedicated to all my fans and the anthologies that originally published many of the short stories upon these pages. Your confidence in my work became my confidence in my writing. Oh, and please remember to wash your hands when you're finished.

A special thanks to Linda Stay of Customer & Media Relations with Squatty Potty© for your immediate support and enthusiasm for this book. And to Dookie, the Squatty Potty© Unicorn, for your brilliant haiku!

Table of Contents
NUMBER ONE – From 0-999 words

NUMBER ONE

Short Stories Under 1,000 Words

SQUATTY POTTY©
DOOKIE THE UNICORN
HAIKU

"OH SQUATTY POTTY
YOU FILL ME WITH ENDLESS JOY
YET LEAVE ME EMPTY."

FOREVER GRAY

She hid in shadows cheating Death, whispering, "I'll be safe amidst the gray."

For years, she shadow-walked evading Grim till everyone she loved was in Death's grasp.

"I surrender," she said, slipping from her screen.

But shadow life had stained her gray.

The Reaper couldn't see her to take.

MCDONALD'S FARM

McDonald sprinted at full speed. His heart raced in his chest as his boots smacked the packed dirt. Sweat soaked through his straw hat. His pursuer shadowed him. She matched him, step for step. He dared not sideglance and give her any advantage.

She already had one.

A claw caught him in the back. He screamed. She paralleled his pitch with vibrato. The ratchet chicken had finally flown the coop. The diva and her entourage of back up chicken singers sang out through beaks stained with red lipstick, "Old McDonald *HAD* a farm," in perfect harmony.

ROADSIDE VENDOR

I drove three counties to try one. Greasy meat cooking from the sidewalk stand, pumped out like an aphrodisiac.

I ordered a double.

"Too late. Sold out."

I stood planted, not going anywhere.

The vendor smiled. "Follow me. I make you special."

He led me to an alley, a side door, a blackout. I came to when my foot hit the grinder; mechanical teeth munching, making me minced meat. The vendor watched.

"I make you special," he repeated.

Wish I'd told someone where I went. But they'll never find me now.

Unless they drive three counties.

And order a double.

ASYLUM OF THE DEAD

Across blimey seas sail the asylum of the dead; lodgers on a passageway to the gates of Hell.

With heavy swords of bone, scabbards encrusted with the jewels of their sins, the treacherous brood fight and kill then rise again, each trying to break free of their own bond.

The ratline is lowered at Hell's gate.

Hellhounds snarl and yelp at the fresh meat.

With laden steps, they climb down the rope through thick blinding fog, only to find they are back on the ships' deck ready to set sail, to kill and be killed; in limbo for all eternity.

PICTURE WINDOW

The dolls lay in heaps on the playroom floor. Broken and tattered, decapitated and fragmented, the lifeless bodies stare blankly through marbled eyes. The room reeks of plastic and fibers. The music box's eerie chorus tinges and twanges off-beat as it slows.

Little Suzie stands over the carnage brandishing a kitchen knife; the serrated teeth worn down to nubs like the gums beneath her grandma's dentures. She doesn't smile as she stares at the massacre on the cashmere throw, her eyes filled with curiosity and intrigue. Light filters through the limbs outside the picture window casting opposing lines of shadows and brilliance upon the bodies.

For a second, Suzie considers cleaning the mess. But the nanny is due any minute and Suzie needs to be back from the kitchen before she returns. The knife is too dull to add the Nanny's body to the others.

THE DEVIL'S STRINGS

I sold my soul to the Devil.

He promised me the world, promised me my dreams in a contract tied closed with his guitar strings. So, I did it. Took his pen and signed my name. Watched my blood spread on the page. He made me a star; made the whole world love me. Crowds chant my name every night, every place. My face covers billboards like graffiti that can't be erased. Number one on the charts, records gone platinum and gold, seems a small price to pay for my soul.

But when the crowd's gone, the hotel rooms look the same, smell the same—shit, they all *taste* the same. I wonder now about the price of fame. And that old Devil is a tricky son of a bitch. He never showed me the fine print, that script beneath the dotted line, how I'd *really* been bound. Bet he knew I wouldn't take the time.

So now, I'm stuck strumming these strings forever.

Cause when I stop, the headaches begin; migraines that pump and rock my mind unless I play that stage each and every night. I can't do it no more. My fingers bleed, have stained those strings. Can't rock; just roll me to sleep.

But the Devil don't care. He knew all along that he'd own not just my soul but the life I'd traded there. Carefully, I toss those strings around my neck, around the beam. And when you find this song, my last to sing, you'll know the contract's been fulfilled.

'Cause I'll be hanging from the Devil's strings.

ALIENATION

There must have been thousands that day, standing in the rain.

Stark grey cityscape with glass buildings looming like giants high in the atmosphere dripped rain to the streets far beneath. Those standing outside held black sheets to block their heads. A sea of blank faces matching those of the expressionless giants surrounding them. One by one, the crowd gathered spreading down alleyways and filling damp corners, unhindered by the downpour. A handful of brave ones lingered atop the skyscrapers, defenseless, holding scribbled cardboard signs exclaiming their welcome or begging for a lift.

Rain hammered from above glistening as falling stardust where my ship's beams reflected off. I scanned the crowd on the flat roofs, bored by the naïve begging departure to unknown places or offering their homes to strangers with secret motives.

I wished I could see those hidden beneath the black tarp, but it was useless.

My mission was clear, and the twin souls I searched for did not stand on a rooftop.

If they walked among the thousands standing in

the rain, I could not find them. And I wasn't paid enough to land and expose myself to these bipedal creatures.

Who knew what they could do to me!

I would have to return another day, when the weather was clear. It amused me to glimpse the disappointment on the alien faces of those holding homemade signs of welcome as they watched me go. What an ignorant race to willingly throw themselves at my mercy without knowing my intentions.

But such was the fascination that kept our kind coming back to the third rock from the sun. We still had many questions about how these creatures were put together, how they could appear identical in form yet retain their own uniqueness, why they did the things they did.

Questions my superiors would await to have answered another day.

BEAKERS & TISSUES

Bertha Jones stared intently into the beaker. The liquid inside had gelled into a clear solution. Very peculiar, Bertha thought. In the matching jacket beside her, as sterile on the inside as she was on the outside, stood Dr. Margarite Fellington, Director and Supreme Being of the Forthcoming Intergalactic Remaking of Life Institute, where Bertha was employed.

It wasn't the greatest job. After all, she had to dissect aliens and remove tissues for specimens all day long. She was searching for the answer to life, but how could she possibly find that among the dead?

Still, a paycheck was a paycheck.

Slowly, Margarite slinked toward her, her beaded glasses hanging like grasping hands around her neck.

Bertha shivered.

"It is not the correct percentage," Margarite snapped, spittle flying from her crooked stained teeth. "You must start from scratch."

Bertha's shoulders hunched. Back to the drawing board.

As Margarite left the room, she paused. Her icy voice came in a whisper, "You will find the answer today or you will be replaced."

And it hit her.

Bertha grabbed the scalpel on the cold metal table and lunged at Dr. Fellington. The blade slipped through haggard skin between her shoulder blades and into the place where her heart should have been.

The witch didn't even flinch.

Margarite turned her head askew and said, "You should not have done that."

She reached behind and slipped the scalpel from her back, the skin and tissues making a suctioning sound, which turned Bertha's stomach. With an inhuman speed and agility, Margarite lunged upon Bertha, and strapped her to the examination table by her wrists and ankles.

"What are you doing?" Bertha screeched.

"Finishing the job."

Bertha felt the cold metal slip into her thigh, her forearm, the side of her head. Tissue samples were collected. Bertha's breathing slowed. Her blood trudged through her veins as mud in a river. She watched the doctor mix her flesh with the solution Bertha had created. And in horror, she saw a smile creep across Dr. Mararite Fellington's decrepit mouth. Bertha's tissues held the answers they were consumed with discovering.

And in her final seconds, she knew, her own death would be the answer for the others' life.

HAVE PATIENTS

Herman Sligo sat in the tweed rocker at Spring Creek Hospital watching re-runs on the television. His nurse, Emily, approached with a smile. "Is this your episode, Herman?"

In response, he dug his finger in his ear.

Fifty years ago, he was a bit actor who played Uncle Emil in three episodes of the popular series *The Five Sisters*. In the fifth season, he exchanged a line with Susie Sizemore, the blonde bombshell that *CBS* brought in to raise ratings. He remembered his line clearly: *Watch the green ones. They're not what you think they are.*

"It's time for your medicine," Emily said, handing him a white pill and a paper cup.

Herman placed the pill on his tongue, forcing it down without water. Emily touched his shoulder and continued her rounds, her hand reminding him of Sophie's.

They had met while Herman was working on *The Five Sisters* and got married in Vegas within the first month. The divorce came after only a year, when Sophie walked in on Herman practicing more that just lines in Suzie Sizemore's trailer.

A loud buzzer sounded and Herman shuffled across the linoleum flooring to his room. The door closed then locked behind him and he stood in the center for some time. A green-framed photograph stood on the nightstand of Uncle Emil with his arm around Susie Sizemore. He just wouldn't leave her alone, no matter how much Herman begged him. Herman saw the bloody knife in the snow and her lifeless body behind the house. He was holding the knife over her when the police arrived.

"She was dead when I found her," he told the cops. "It was Uncle Emil!"

But Uncle Emil was nowhere to be found, except on those three episodes that Herman couldn't find anywhere. The only proof that could clear his name.

A slot in his door slid open and a guard set a Styrofoam tray on the ledge. "Dinner time," he said.

Herman did not answer as he reached for his tray noticing Easter jelly-beans in one of the cups. He popped in a yellow one, expecting to taste lemon, but banana cream pie coated his tongue.

The guard smiled. "Watch the green ones," he said, walking away. "They're not what you think they are."

In that moment, something snapped and Herman Sligo disappeared beneath the role of Uncle Emil until his final season would come to an end.

And no one but Herman even noticed.

ABSOLUTION

"I know why you did it," Lawrence said, picking at his cuticles. "And truthfully, I don't blame you."

The man sitting across from Lawrence crossed his plump hands on the cold, metal table; the clink from his handcuffs like the gavel that put them there.

"I'd have done it myself, if I wasn't afraid of jail time."

Lawrence looked up at the man who no longer wore his convictions in a small white square upon his neck. He smiled. "I bet you're wondering why I'm here, Father. Can I still call you that? I can't help but call you that. It's what you've always been to me."

The priest stared with steel gray eyes the way he probably did all those times behind the mesh wall in his confessional, only now Lawrence could see them, feel them. This was, after all, a final confession.

Wasn't it?

"I guess it just seems wrong, you know?" Lawrence stammered. "That you're in here when it should be me."

The priest covered his eyes, his face, and began to weep. After some time, he reached out to Lawrence.

Lawrence had completed his penance.

A buzzer sounded. The guard reappeared and opened the heavy steel door. Tears slipped from Lawrence's eyes. The priest released him and stood, his walk stunted by shackled feet.

"I'm sorry, Father!" Lawrence called, as the priest left without a word, leaving Lawrence alone with hands stained by unseen blood.

In twelve hours, Father Rose would sit in the electric chair. His hands and feet staked. His head crowned in electric thorns. His soul forever separated from God. His faith replaced with revulsion.

Lawrence would watch the priest calmly sit, like a sacrificial lamb led to the slaughter, and die for his sins. Sins that were not the priest's to carry.

But he would anyway.

And in the afterlife, Lawrence knew he would pay for what he had done.

Lawrence stood, wiped his face dry, and left the small visiting room. He was too prideful to go to prison. He was only nine when the arrest occurred all those years ago. He had his whole life ahead of him.

The priest had already lived his life.

They both made their choices. Father Rose made his when he impregnated a young girl and brought a bastard son into the world. Lawrence made his when he pulled the trigger. He couldn't let her tell anyone the truth. And when she threatened to contact the Vatican, the decision came easy.

Only the priest knew it was Lawrence who had pulled the trigger. And only Lawrence knew the priest's confession was a lie. After all, a father's job was to protect his son.

TURNING

I crouch in the alley corner, panting, heaving, my body drenched, like with night sweats. The dark alley reeks of vomit and urine. I am surrounded by puddles of sewage, black flies, and lights flickering on and off.

I know *It* is with me. Though I can't see *It*, I can feel *It*, like a thought on the tip of my tongue. I shiver—no, convulse—in violent agitations. I am so thirsty. What the fuck is going on? I need to get out of here. But *It* won't let me leave.

My muscles feel atrophied. How long have I been here? With what little strength I have, I push myself up against the wall. Pain sears through my leg. I look down. My leg is broken, but I can't remember how it happened. Still, I have to move.

I crawl over to the fire escape ladder like a wounded animal, dragging my gimpy leg in a stupor, the pain pushing me toward blacking out. But I can't collapse or *It* will overtake me. And I know *It* is watching, waiting.

Grabbing the bottom rung of the ladder, I lift myself to my feet. I limp along at first, like I'm drunk, but find it becomes easier and easier to move. The convulsions have passed; I am no longer sweating. I bolt toward the street, pulling my leg as deadweight.

The street is worn and quiet. Where is everyone? Has it always been this way? No, I remember a time when it was different. When I didn't feel *It* breathing down my neck. I have a wife. But where is she?

Lurching down the main street I try to cry out, my throat too dry to make any sound. I hear guttural noises, grunting, retching, and I know *It* is closer, closing in on me.

I have a son, too. And, somehow I know he is gone. I hear him crying. No, that's now.

The crying.

There is a boy out here. I have to save him. I have to find him, before *It* finds him. I quicken my step, my twisted leg lagging uselessly behind. It no longer hurts. The blood inside me is thick, coagulating in my veins like gelatin. My thirst is turning to hunger.

I'm getting closer to the boy His crying echoes off the walls and slams against my eardrums. *It* is closer, too, retching and grunting.

"Shut up," I try to yell. "It will hear you."

But I can't.

I find the boy curled in a ball between two trash dumps. Screaming. I near the boy, his eyes wide with terror, his voice so shrill it makes my ears bleed.

"Run!" I want to yell. "It's here!"

But no words leave my mouth. My arm swings out, hooking the boy. He tries breaking free. I don't blame him. But it's over for him. It's over for us both.

A tear forms, which never leaves my eye.

I bend over to whisper in his ear; to tell him I'm sorry, to remember what a boy smells like, to remember my son. Instead, *It* consumes him, ripping out his neck and devouring his flesh as I just stand there, watching, unable to stop myself.

WHY THERE ARE MORE HOT DOGS THAN BUNS
A FABLE

A long, long time ago, Lord Kensington and Lady Buttermilk met on a beautiful spring day. Chirping birds showered them in song. The sun sprayed them in brilliant diamonds. And the air kissed their blushed cheeks. Never in the history of time had a couple been more in love than this. What of Romeo and Juliet, you may ask? Friends in comparison. Bella Swan and Edward Cullen? Mere strangers.

After many years of courting, they married. The entire kingdom attended the extravagant ceremony. The Lady's cake was seventeen stories high, a replica of the Lord's castle, studded in precious gems and spring flowers, "Like the ones in bloom on the day we met," she had told the baker. Her seamstress layered lace upon chiffon to create an immaculate gown detailed with eloquent beadwork and handspun silk. Her dress far surpassed the rags procured by the Fairy Godmother for Cinderella.

At the reception, Lord Kensington provided banquet platters filled with the cylindrical meat he had patented and built his fortune upon; *Dogs of Heat*, named after the way his dachshund looked when he stretched in the summer sun. But Lady Buttermilk had a surprise for her new husband. She personally had toiled for months in the kitchen kneading elongated pastry dough into lengthened bread, which she called *buns*, to hold the Lord's meat. "This way," she told Lord Kensington, "the people will no longer scorch their bare hands on your *Dogs of Heat.*"

The combination was magnanimous, an overnight sensation, and soon every village marketplace sold *Dogs of Heat* and *buns* in separate packages containing ten of each. "One for each of the ten Kensington Lords, in which my lineage is rooted," Lord Kensington explained.

"Or perhaps, my Lord," Lady Buttermilk interjected, "it will be one for each of the ten sons I will bare for your Lordship."

Lord Kensington seemed troubled after this, although the Kingdom flourished financially. The news quickly spread across the land and to the four corners of the earth that Lord Kensington's *Dogs of Heat* and Lady Buttermilk's *buns* were the greatest combination since red wine and oranges.

Merchants arrived by foot, horseback, and sea to purchase packages to carry back to their land, and every one received equally paired sacks of ten *Dogs of Heat* and ten *buns* to be sure no one scorched their bare hands while eating.

One day, on a routine weekend trip to visit the various farmlands providing Lady Buttermilk with flour, sugar, and the other ingredients she used to bake *buns*, she was forced to return home suddenly after a peasant woman gave her an apple, which brought forth food poisoning.

Upon her early return, Lady Buttermilk caught Lord Kensington in the carnal act with the Lady's own handmade, the curvaceous and devious Staabs Backsalot. A brutal divorce followed, and the Lady was able to not only retain ownership of her patent on *buns*, but she also managed to gain legal possession of his Lordship's *Dogs of Heat*, which she quickly shortened to *Hot Dogs* to avoid brand confusion. She changed the packaging, placing ten *Hot Dogs* in a case, but only eight *buns* per bag, leaving everyone who purchased a set with two extra *Hot Dogs* that would scorch their bare hands.

And to this day, hot dogs and buns are sold in mismatched numbers, leaving two extra dogs every time.

* * *

And the moral of the story is don't screw with the woman who holds your buns, or you'll be left holding your wiener in your bare hands.

WHITE-WATER

They done told me there's a well for white folk only on this farm, and that us Negroes ain't allowed to drink no white-water. It all looks the same to me, the water I mean, clear and crisp, coming from God's green earth. So, who's to say which is white-water and which ain't? I still don't know. I ain't nobody's fool. I never had no schooling, but I learnt my A-B-Cs as a kid, most of them, at any rate. The ones I need to read the word *Negro* and *White* so I know which bathroom I supposed to do my business in.

I heard the preacher giving sermons, how there ain't no Jew or gentile, no freeman or slave no more. It sure as heck-fire ain't that way where I live. No, sir. We Negroes still slaves, even though the shackles been long gone.

But I was thirsty that day, see? And there weren't no place to drink from, like I'd been told. So, I asked the Boss Man, I said, "Please, boss. Pardon ya for a drink?" And he don't pay me no mind. Just shoo me back to the field to pick his harvest; mouth curled in a sneer of tobacco-stained teeth, drooling black out the edges like some dang rabid coon needs putting down.

It was so hot that day, hotter than any harvest day I been used to and I asked Boss Man, real kind-like, about half a dozen times, for even a mouthful of his white-water.

"None for you," Boss Man said. "This is for white folk, not Negroes."

Coulda been the heat, made me do it. Or coulda been I was just so thirsty, I ain't been able to think straight. But after awhile, I don't remember much why. Don't think it matters none neither.

After sunset, after Boss Man had his supper and I ate me some stale cornbread and a bowlful of black-eyed peas without a lick of water to wash them down, I grabbed me a thick branch that's been smoothed, and dipped it in the tar bucket. Marched up to the fire pit, and set that black glob of tar on fire. I passed the white-water well, but didn't stop for no drink. Couldn't. Boss Man said, "No," and I ain't the type to disobey my master. I went over to Boss Man's quarters, where I seen him smoking his cigar. He's passed out on the front porch from drinking too much moonshine. Figured I'd ask him one more time. Even if'n he's too drunk to answer.

I was just so thirsty.

His eyes popped real big in the flame light as I poured his moonshine all over him. I saw the understanding sink in, and I knew then he'd wished he'd shared his white-water with me.

But it was too late.

"If that's your water," I told him, "then I gotta make it right for Negroes. You gotta understand, Boss, that we all the same. That's what the Bible says."

I touched the flame to him, watched him light

up like a shooting star, and run cross the yard, through the field, burning half his own dang harvest to the ground. When I found him midway in the clearing, his skin charred and black as mine, I told him, "Now we equal, boss. Now we the same. So, it's okay if we is drinking from the same well."

I tipped my hat to him, like my grandma taught me to always do when passing a white man, and I went back to the well, where I ladled me a big scoop of water and took a long drink. And you know what? For the first time in a long while, I believed what the Good Book said.

And I felt free.

BACKSEAT DRIVER

Mark plugged in the new GPS unit. Static hummed through the speakers. The guy at Radio Shack had guaranteed *The Sergeant* would provide excellent guidance and direction. Bloody-well better, at the price Mark had paid for it. *The Sergeant* was voice activated and able to communicate on the spot, altering its conversation to each owner.

"Let's give it a shot," Mark said, turning over the engine.

The Sergeant was quiet.

Mark cleared his throat. "I'd like directions to the nearest bar."

Nothing happened. Not a blip. Not a beep. Not a word.

Mark enunciated, "Dir-ections-to-the-near-est-bar."

Silence.

"Great." Mark reached for the door handle as the Radio Shack sign dimmed and the lights turned off. He pounded on the glass door, but no one answered. Mark stormed back to his Buick, peeled out, and hopped onto the highway.

Suddenly, *The Sergeant* lit up. "Private, exactly

where do you think you're going?"

Mark smirked. "Just driving."

"You will address me as 'Sir. Yes, Sir!' is that clear, Private?"

Mark stared at the green camo box attached to his dash.

"PRIVATE!"

"Sir. Yes, Sir!"

"Good. There's hope for you yet."

The car continued down the dark, two-way highway. Not another car in sight. Mark's palms sweat.

"Switch lanes, Private."

"But that's the oncoming traffic lane."

"Are you questioning my orders?" *The Sergeant* screeched.

Mark swerved over. "Sir. No, Sir!"

"You leave the thinking to me, you spineless excuse for a driver!"

Ahead, the distant lamps of a semi rounded the bend. *The Sergeant* was silent. The semi approached. The truck flicked the headlights on and off. Mark swerved back into his lane.

"Jesus H. Christ, Private. What the hell are you doing?"

"Are you serious?"

"Did I or did I not give you a direct order?"

"You did, but—"

"And you decided, like the scum that you are, to disobey my order."

Mark was speechless. Was this really happening?

"Did you suck on your mama's titty for too long? Did you look at her one day and realize it was time to see other people? Or do you still dream of suckling her milk-maker when you lie alone in the dark?"

Mark listened to *The Sergeant's* heavy breathing. It sounded so real. So alive.

"You move when I tell you to move."

The car swerved back into the tractor trailer's lane. Mark yanked on the unyielding steering wheel.

"I will not tolerate insubordination, even if that Jezebel of a mother of yours did. Do you understand me, Private?"

"Come on, man!"

"You will not eat or take a leak without my permission. You belong to me now, you worthless swine!"

An air horn blared through the still night air.

"Where'd you learn to drive, scum?" *The Sergeant* berated. "Did you find your driver's license at the bottom of a Cracker Jacks box?"

The horn blasted in alarm.

"Please!" Mark screamed.

"Answer the question!"

"Sir. No, Sir!"

As the semi drew close enough for Mark to make out the dark features on the driver's face, *The Sergeant* pulled the Buick into the correct lane; the semi passed before Mark's eyes as a blur.

"Jesus Christ," Mark whispered.

"Now," *The Sergeant* said, "do we have an understanding?"

Mark's heart hammered in his chest. Adrenaline coursed with the rising and falling of the RPMs. "Sir. Yes. Sir."

"Good. At the road up ahead turn right."

Mark spied the opening to the dirt access road. "But—"

The Sergeant forced the accelerator to the floorboard.

"Sir. Yes, Sir!" Mark flicked his turn signal to emphasize his commitment.

The Sergeant released the gas pedal.

The road neared. Mark turned. Trees towered as guardians on either side of the one-lane pass, bearers of the dark deeds that transpired beneath them. Mark couldn't see more than a few feet ahead on the bumpy path. A fog rolled in.

"What are you?" Mark asked.

"The Sergeant."

"What do you want with me?"

"My only obsession in life is to take you from the worthless maggot that you are and make you into a man. Isn't that what you want, Private?"

Chills crossed the back of Mark's neck. The doors locked. The headlamps burned out.

"Please let me go!"

The lights turned back on.

"Turn left here," *The Sergeant* directed.

Mark angled the car and drove into the expanse of trees for several yards until he came to a ledge. He slammed the brakes. "Why are you doing this?"

"Not everyone is cut out for the Corps, Son. I'm afraid we're going to have to let you go."

Mark began to whimper.

"Drive, Private."

"No!"

"DRIVE!" *The Sergeant* said as a choking heat flooded the car. "No one will miss you. They won't even notice you're gone until your rent is past due. Your useless life will end tonight."

Pain swelled in Mark's chest as the car slipped into gear.

"When they finally do ask, I'll let them know the truth."

Slowly, the car edged forward. Mark's eyes widened in terror as his own foot compressed the accelerator.

The Sergeant whispered the truth Mark was afraid to say aloud as Mark screamed.

"The devil made me do it," *The Sergeant* said.

To which Mark replied, "Sir. Yes, Sir."

NUMBER TWO

Short Stories from 1,000-5,000 Words

AS FATE WOULD HAVE IT

The cave-in happened on a Saturday in the fall of 1891. I remember it like it was yesterday. It was cool outside with a light drizzle and the dampness beat through my flannel shirt like an *Ex-* ignoring a restraining order. Old man Lido led our crew, barking out orders like we were a team of sled dogs. The rumbling started just before lunch. I looked around. No one seemed to notice; Chuck and John still shoveling by the pound, Mighty Mike wheeling out the carts.

I worked the Kentucky coal mines for years, breathing in coal dust like it was some forgotten element of the periodic table. At my age I still haven't developed the black lung, even though I smoke like a chimney.

Kind of wish I would.

I meant to leave early that day. Would have missed the disaster by minutes if I had. But I was there, standing outside the cave and I heard everything. My crew screamed for help from their black tomb, sealed off from the outside world until all the oxygen was gone and their voices gradually quieted. I still hear them screaming when I close my eyes, crying out for help until I black out when Jim silences them.

"You could have saved us," they tell me. "You could have saved us."

And I could have.

I stumble upstairs to my bedroom with Jim, the bottle nearly gone, the voices still there.

"I'm sorry," is all I can say, as I do every time.

Why was my life spared? Me, a con-man by age sixteen, wanted in three states for forgery and robbery; an orphan who never understood love or home. The closest I came were the dirty hotel rooms where I'd hold whores until I'd cum then make them leave.

Things weren't supposed to be this way.

I drop to the edge of the bed, fumble with my old boot laces and manage to get one off before giving up and flopping down on the bare mattress. The night creeps in through the open window; a coal-black nothingness that fills my room.

"Why?" Mighty Mike screams. "Why'd ya do it?"

I can see him standing there with the cart in his black hands, his body in late stages of decay.

"I had no choice," I say. "I swear it."

The darkness grows heavy, weighing down on my chest; tons of coal suffocating me.

"You stole my family," Chuck howls, shovel in hand, blue circles framing his eyes.

"I know," I say, "I'm sorry!"

"You did this to me," John accuses with a pointing finger, his pale skin translucent in death.

"I'm sorry," I whisper, barely able to breathe.

The air grows stifling and still. Pressure keeps

me pinned to the bed and I'm gasping now in pure blackness.

"Help!" I scream, though the word never leaves my mouth.

I writhe around on the bed, try to break free, manage to roll myself over and drop to the floor. I claw at the hardwood and my nails, still stained black from the mines, bend and splinter leaving a blood trail in their wake. Spinning laughter traps me inside my head.

The spinning voices of my crew.

My mouth fills with dust I can't spit out and I gag. Blackness fills my throat, cutting off my air – choking me.

"I'm sorry," I mouth as my burning lungs give in.

My heartbeat slows from the sludge passing through my veins. I am dying in the cave-in, in my room; the single act of vengeance by the apparitions who have haunted me for over ninety years.

When will it end? I wonder. *Why have they waited so long?*

I imagine someone finds me dead in a couple weeks, when the scent of my corpse is strong enough to alert the neighbors. Find an old man who drank himself to death, alone, with no one to mourn him.

But what no one knows is that I died that Saturday in the cave-in, along with my crew, so there won't be any corpse to bury.

I'd taken out life insurance policies on all of them, Mighty Mike, John and Chuck, before I rigged the explosives, planning to use the money to pay off a hefty gambling debt then hightail it to Mexico. The charge went off early. I was still inside.

But Fate didn't like that and bargained with the Reaper to let me live. So I alone walked out of that mine, charred but alive. I didn't pay off the debt. Instead, I kept the money and started a new life across the border.

I'll be one-hundred and twelve next spring. But every fall, on the Saturday of the cave-in, I die again in the rubble, and each time I hear the voices of the men I killed haunt me and there's nothing I can do to make them go away – not even by trying to drink and smoke myself to death – not even by sending money to their widows all these years... not even by getting too old to still be living.

I don't know how long Fate bargained to let me live. All I know is the Reaper's not coming for me anytime soon, but I have to believe he will come. I can't go on this way forever. Maybe, after I live long enough to fill four lifetimes, I will have made amends to my crew for what I've done to them. And after all that, maybe Fate will be satisfied and let Grim finally come reap me for all that I have sown.

CAUC BOY

In the quiet city of Melbourne, Florida, somewhere along Highway One, sits the small office of a mild-mannered realtor named Jason Eagle. Unbeknownst to most are his true intentions, his deepest secrets sealed beneath his hidden identity: he is the Caucasian Lover, a.k.a. *Cauc Boy*. A mighty vessel which no woman can resist, Cauc Boy has but two weaknesses: Janine and hot chicken wings.

"Cauc Boy, you're my hero," Janine says.

"I know," Cauc Boy answers. "Do you smell chicken wings?"

"Oh, Cauc Boy." And they share just one kiss.

But then, one day….

It is slow in the real estate market. Not many buyers and too many sellers. Jason is sitting on his throne…doing his business, when he hears a desperate cry for help with his super-sonic hearing.

Somewhere, a woman is crying. And by the sound of it, she must be beautiful.

"Help! Help!"

Quickly, Jason finishes his business, and rips off his shirt. Oh no! He forgot his Cauc Boy costume at the dry cleaners.

After running twelve blocks to the dry cleaners, getting money from the ATM, then paying the bill, he finds an empty phone booth – which is really hard when everyone uses cell phones – and leaps out, emerging as Cauc Boy, ready for action.

He flies to the scene, a small coffee shop in Cocoa Village, where he sees a beautiful woman – just as he suspected – crying at an outdoor table under an umbrella, a frothed cappuccino spilled across her paperwork.

"No use crying over frothed milk," Cauc Boy says, reaching out his hand.

The beautiful woman looks up. "But my papers, how will I ever get my profile right for the online dating service when I can't write on them?"

"Don't worry about that. They will be dried out in no time."

Cauc Boy picks her up and sets her at a new, clean table. "What is your name?"

"Neida Love."

With his hands on his hips, he concentrates and puckers up, blowing hot air across the table where she sits. The cappuccino peels off the paperwork and spills back into the mug, which is turned upright again, the top frothing with foam and piping hot.

Cauc Boy stops blowing. Steam rises from the full mug.

"Who are you?"

"I am Cauc Boy. You make sure to be more careful from now on when you're drinking hot beverages. You could get burned that way."

Neida Love lowers her head. "I've been burned before."

Cauc Boy lifts her chin. "I believe your luck might be turning." He smiles. "But now, I must go. The Cauc is needed elsewhere." With a great leap, Cauc Boy zooms through the air and flies out of sight.

Neida Love watches him disappear in the clouds. "Cauc Boy. My hero."

Cauc Boy reaches his office in Melbourne and notices the parking lot is empty. "No need to change back into my work clothes. I think I'll go spend the rest of the day with my first love, Janine. And my second love, a plate of hot chicken wings." He pauses. "Maybe I'll get the chicken wings first." And he flies off to the nearest Wild Wings.

Meanwhile....

In an art gallery in downtown Melbourne, a slinky man dressed in black slacks and matching turtleneck steals priceless art from the *almost* famous Cliffton Chandelier. As the art thief escapes down the stairs, he lets out a maniacal laugh. "No one can stop me now."

Suddenly, Cauc Boy's cell phone rings. It is Cliffton Chandelier.

"Grady Taste has just stolen all my artwork, and I have a huge exhibition tonight! Can you help?"

Cauc Boy wipes hot sauce from his lips and grabs Janine into his arms for a long steamy kiss. "Cliffton, I'll be there in ten minutes."

"Gotta go?" Janine asks, with a pout.

"Duty calls," Cauc Boy replies. "You have to share the Cauc with everyone. But my heart belongs only to you."

Janine smiles as Cauc Boy leaps into the air, flying toward Downtown Melbourne.

Over the shops and pubs, Cauc Boy searches for

his greatest nemesis, Grady Taste. Once a savvy art collector and well-respected member of the art community, Grady Taste was dumped by his one true love and began stealing artwork. No one really understands the connection, exactly.

In the darkest shadows of the buildings, Cauc Boy, using his heat-sensing vision, finds Grady Taste and quickly flies down to apprehend him.

Before Grady Taste can sketch an escape, Cauc Boy scoops him up while grabbing the stolen artwork with his free hand. He flies the kicking and screaming criminal back to Downtown Melbourne where Cliffton Chandelier awaits outside his gallery.

Grady Taste hands back the art. "I'm sorry, Cliffton."

"Why did you do it?" Cliffton asks.

"I don't really know why, exactly. Ever since my one true love dumped me, I just thought stealing art would make me feel better." He looks up. Clifton and Cauc Boy stare puzzled. "I don't really understand the connection, either."

Placing his arm around Grady's shoulder, Cauc Boy says, "I know exactly what you need." With a leap, Cauc Boy is off again, carrying Grady Taste by the scruff of his neck.

"No! Please don't take me back to the print store in the mall. I'll do anything!"

The two descend upon the veranda of a coffee shop in Cocoa Village. A beautiful woman is reading a book; a pile of brown, stained papers litter the table beside her.

"Neida Love?" Cauc Boy says.

She looks up. "Yes?"

"This is Grady Taste."

"How do you do?" Neida Love says.

Grady Taste offers a small smile and a nervous nod.

"He's a big art fan," Cauc Boy adds.

"Really," Neida Love says. "Me, too."

As Grady Taste and Neida Love get acquainted, Cauc Boy watches for a moment. "My work here is done," he says with a sigh and flies away.

Later that evening, Janine and Jason attend Cliffton Chandelier's art exhibition where he has finally sold his last piece.

"This couldn't have happened without Cauc Boy," Cliffton announces.

"I'll be sure and tell him," Jason says. "That's what the Cauc is for."

Janine leads Jason into a secluded back room inside the gallery.

"You sure had your hands full today, Cauc Boy."

"But never too full for you," Jason says, grabbing Janine and pulling her in close for a kiss.

As the door closes, Janine says, through the darkness, "Cauc Boy. My hero."

BLACK FRIDAY

The Clay family had been waiting in line since Tuesday. Now, here it was, Thursday eve, and the line had just started to move. The chapel bells pealed their cries of midnight, the beginning of a new day, Black Friday, and everyone was itching to get out of the cold and into the warmth of the chapel.

Martha Sprinkle stood near the front of the line, her straw-colored hair pinned beneath a brand new bonnet. She turned back, looking at Corra with a stare that would have caused a snake to shed its skin.

Corra bit at her bare cuticles, drawing blood. She was mousy, that's how she'd always been described by adults, and the boys passed her by the way they did an oak, without a second glance.

"Come, Corra," Regina Clay prompted, taking a step in the line.

Corra shuffled her feet behind her mother, kicking up dirt in puffs.

"Watch it, stupid," Raymond Jr. blasted. "You're getting shit all over my boots." He pushed his sister from behind and Corra stumbled, bumping into Martha who let out a shriek.

"Corra Clay, you have to be the clumsiest girl I've

ever met," she said.

"At least I ain't stuck on myself," Corra mumbled, which was met by glares from both her mother and brother.

"Now serving seventy-three," the man with the mustache announced from the town square.

Corra looked at the crumpled paper in her hands, the number seventy-seven scripted in perfect calligraphy.

"I'm getting a beautiful new China doll with a red silk dress covered in roses," Martha beamed.

Her parents beamed back, her father adding, "Bet it won't look more beautiful than you, darling."

"Of course not," Raymond Jr. chimed in. "You're the most beautiful girl in the whole town."

Corra made a gagging sound, met by more glares from her family, including an awful one from Martha that made her face scrunch up and turn crimson. Corra smiled, happy to see she had wiped the pretty right off Martha's face.

"Now serving seventy-five."

In small steps, the line herded forward, like cattle being led to the slaughter. Corra glimpsed at her ticket again. The number hadn't changed.

"What would you get?" Martha asked Raymond Jr., her cobalt eyes round and lifted, her lips glossy and pursed.

Raymond Jr. ran his fingers through the back of his dark hair and shrugged. "I don't know. I'd like a fresh saddle and pistol, maybe even some new spurs for my boots."

Martha giggled, as if Corra's brother had said something interesting. Corra huffed and plopped down in the dirt.

"Corra Jane!" her mother screeched.

Corra's heart went dead in her chest.

"You stand up this instant!" Regina grabbed Corra by the arm, yanking her so hard Corra thought her joint might snap. "Now wipe off your dress. You don't want to be a mess inside the chapel."

Corra wiped off her butt, catching Martha staring at her in disgust. When her mother wasn't looking, Corra gave Martha the middle finger. Martha's jaw gaped and she turned her back to Corra. With a sneer, Corra swatted off the last of the dirt.

"Now serving seventy-six," the announcer stated.

Martha faced her parents, hugged them both, then kissed them on the cheeks. "I hope this years harvest is plentiful," she said. She looked back at Raymond Jr., but her eyes had changed. They were wide, her long lashes brushing her upper lids, and the look inside of them sent chills straight through the marrow in Corra's bones.

Corra jerked around. "I don't wanna go in. I don't want anything. No dolls, no dresses, not toys. Nothing."

Her mother's face blanched, as if Corra had just taken the Lord's name in vain.

"I hate Black Friday," Corra continued in a rant. "Don't make me go. Don't make me do it, Mama."

"What's the matter with you?" Raymond Jr. asked, placing his arms around Regina's frail shoulders. "You're scarring Mama."

Corra's face flushed. "Scarring *Mama*? What about *me*?"

Regina sobbed gently, pulling a handkerchief from

her handbag. "Now, Corra," she said. "This isn't about you. It's about the harvest." She wiped her nose. "This is the season of giving, and you will sacrifice like every other girl your age. Now, stop talking nonsense, and think about what you want for Black Friday."

Corra's heart burned a hole in her chest as her shoulders slumped forward. "I'm sorry, Mama. I don't want you upset."

Composing herself, Regina forced a small smile. "Atta girl," she said, pushing a strand of Corra's blonde hair behind her ear. "Just think of all the great treasures you'll receive after giving of yourself."

Corra looked into Regina's gray eyes. There was nothing left to say.

"Your father would be so proud of you."

"Now serving number seventy-seven."

Regina wiped away her tears, pulling her daughter in for a hug. "You'll do fine."

Corra nodded numbly.

"Try not to screw this up," Raymond Jr. said, punching Corra in the arm.

Corra stepped past her family through the stained glass doors of the chapel. Candlelight spilled across her path. Her shoes tapped across the marble, the noise muffled in the tapestries hanging off the walls like burial shrouds. A man wearing an ornate robe and pointed hat stood on a platform at the center of the room. Beside him, two shirtless boys wearing cargo pants held silver trays; one empty, one littered with glimmering objects Corra could not make out.

With her heart pounding deafeningly loud in her head, Corra approached the man with labored breath and forced steps. She reached the platform, her body trembling. The man motioned for her to kneel and Corra obeyed. *This isn't about you,* Regina's voice echoed.

"I welcome you on this Black Friday," the man stated, "and offer you penance toward God. In return, you will be rewarded for your sacrifice with a gift of your choosing." He stared down with blank eyes. "Well, my dear? What have you chosen?" His pinched words rang shrill, piercing her ears.

"I…I don't know, yet," Corra said.

The man tilted his head, the point of his hat askew, reminding Corra of a Christmas star on a leaning tree. "Well, this is a first. But I suppose you can figure that out along the way."

The man motioned to the boy at his right hand. He looked no older than Corra, maybe twelve-years-old, and as he stepped closer, Corra gasped. His mouth had been sewn shut. The boy bent low and the man chose a knife with a long blade from the ones on the tray.

"Lean forward," the man said.

Corra began to cry, but obeyed.

It's about the harvest.

The second boy knelt before Corra—his lips also sewn closed—and set his silver tray beneath her. Corra's reflection taunted her from the polished silver. Her tears splattered upon it, blurring her image. Through the silver, Corra watched the man raise the knife into the air.

The boys hummed eerie chants.

"For a bountiful harvest," the man said. "May this child be received."

Corra felt the cold blade strike her neck. Ice sliced through her spine and spindled down her nerves. Blood mixed with her tears on the tray, which moved closer, closer, ever closer, until her mind went blank; her death securing a plentiful harvest for her village on this, Corra's last, Black Friday.

ENGLISH CHANNEL

Rachel arrived in a flash of bright light, unsure exactly where she was. Still, she smiled. She had survived the initial test phase of the Trans Aero Commuting Launcher. Her future was solid, and her name would go down in history as the first woman to ever teleport across oceans and continents. But even in her excitement, she couldn't help but notice the ping resonating in her gut that something wasn't right.

Clinging to the nearby fire escape, Rachel steadied, then hobbled out of the alley and down the empty street. Not a single car rolled by. No neon lights or street lamps illuminated the darkness. Faintly, laughter drifted from somewhere up ahead and Rachel crossed the lonely city to find someone.

The laughter brought her to the brick façade of a pub with a green awning the color of pine needles. Piano music rambled out through the small glass panes of the door, along with the rambunctious singing of patrons who must have been drinking for some time. It reminded her of the Old English drinking songs she had seen reenacted in films on her teleport. She took in a deep breath while pressing her gloved hand to the door; the rusty hinges alerted everyone of her entrance.

She wondered why the bar owner didn't use rust resistant coating like building codes demanded. Rachel wanted to turn and leave, realizing too late that this dump was in the wrong part of town, but she was in too far.

The music stopped. The patrons turned from their drinks. The bartender moved closer to his musket leaning against the back wall as painted ladies in nothing but corsets and pantaloons drew away from Rachel, clinging close to those who had bought them for the night. A group of men eyed her from head to toe, the liquor in their blood pulsing immoral thoughts through their heads.

Rachel knew she looked freakishly out of place wearing the metallic gold body suit reflecting the room. She cleared her throat. "Excuse me. I'm looking for Dr. Monroe."

No one responded, as if the voice came from a haunting apparition they could see for the first time.

"Does anyone know Dr. Monroe?" She held the quiver in her throat at bay.

Something was wrong. Something was very wrong.

"There's no doctor in town by such a name," an elderly woman said, eyeing her with suspicion.

Rachel shook her head. "There must be some mistake. I was supposed to meet Dr. Monroe."

"I can be Dr. Monroe," said a man wearing a tricorn hat atop scraggily hair like the tip of a giraffe's tail. He smiled showing tobacco stained teeth and many holes where more had been. "I can be whoever you want me to be, sweetheart."

Rachel forced a smile. "Listen, I'm obviously in the wrong place."

"You can say that again," said one of the painted ladies whose robust bosom fell out of her lace corset.

"Who ya lookin' for again?" the old woman asked.

"Dr. Vincent Monroe."

"Well, you must just be in the wrong public house." The bartender wiped sweat off his brow. "Try the next town over."

"Where am I now?"

"London, love," said the elderly woman.

Rachel's eyes squinted. "This is where I'm supposed to be." She pulled out a hard chair and sat.

"Would you care for some water?" the woman asked.

"Yes," Rachel said, her throat dry from molecular travel.

The bartender took a pitcher and poured Rachel a drink with shaking hands. The woman took it giving him a look, and placed it before Rachel. "Here you are."

Rachel cringed at the clouded water swirling in the glass. A layer of grit settled on the bottom, but she gulped it down anyway. Many patrons seemed to lose interest, returning to their rum and card games, though a few still looked over their shoulders every now and then just in case.

"What's your name?" the elderly woman asked.

"Rachel Watson."

"I'm Tess." She sat for a while, staring at Rachel. "Forgive me, but you don't look as if you're from around here."

"I'm not."

"No. I mean you look as though you're from far, far away from here."

"Like a sexy goddess," the man missing teeth shouted, rolling his tongue across his cracked lips.

"Where'd ya come from?" Tess asked.

"Houston."

Tess's eyes turned down. "Is that somewhere in Greece?"

Rachel laughed. "No. Houston, Texas."

That didn't ring any bells.

"I'm from America."

"Oh," Tess said. "So, you're a colonist. Far from port, ain't ya?"

"A colonist?" Rachel really looked around the pub. Dull earth tones. No electronics or electricity. She threw her attention back to Tess. "What year is it?"

Tess cackled. "Why, what sort of a question is that?"

"It's the kind of question a girl in a gold suit asks when she's accused of being a sexy goddess."

Tess stopped cackling. "It's seventeen-sixty-three."

Rachel's heart skipped as she shook her head. "That can't be." Static hissed in her ears, and Rachel covered them. Somehow her commlink had come back to life.

When she had volunteered to be the guinea pig to teleport for Clarke Innovations, Dr. Clarke insisted a small communication device be implanted in her ear drum to insure it wouldn't come loose during travel. Rachel had never been happier for this decision.

"Rachel?"

"Dr. Clarke," she said with a smile.

"Who are you talking to?" Tess asked, not hearing the other end of the conversation.

Rachel waved her off and hurried out of the pub. "Am I ever glad to hear your voice."

"We lost your capsulization device on the teleboard. Is everything okay?"

"I'm alive, if that's what you mean."

"Did you connect with Dr. Monroe?"

"He's not here."

There was silence on the other end.

"Hello? Dr. Clarke?"

"I'm here. Dr. Monroe is waiting for you at the port cortex and says you have yet to arrive. Are you in London?"

"Yes."

"I don't understand. What happened?"

"You sent me back three-hundred years. This wasn't exactly what I was thinking when you said I'd go down in history."

The commlink sputtered, then silenced.

"Dr. Clarke?"

More static.

"Hello? Are you there?"

Finally, Dr. Clarke responded. "Yes, Rachel. I'm here." After a short pause, he said, "This could take several hours to fix. But don't worry. I'll have the whole team working on it and contact you as soon as it's repaired, okay?"

He didn't sound convincing.

"Sure, doctor," Rachel said, as her commlink silenced.

In the stillness of the night, Rachel stared up into the sky at the many stars glittering above. They were beautiful, without distracting city lights to mute them. Rachel realized some of these stars weren't visible in her night sky back home. Some of them had died so long ago that their last light had burned out before she had a chance to see them. "Kinda like me," she guessed. "Burning here, right now, but from somewhere else altogether." She turned and walked back into the pub, taking an empty seat at the bar beside Tess.

"It seems I could be here a while."

"Well, in that case, let's have a drink. A real one."

"I'd like that," Rachel said smiling.

"Edmund, two rums," Tess told the bartender.

He nodded, grabbed a bottle from the shelf, and three shot glasses. Setting them on the bar top, he poured rum for the three of them.

Tess lifted her glass. "To the colonists who hold a promising future."

"To the future," Rachel said, her glass clinking against Tess's and Edmund's. "May it come sooner than we think."

THE PHOENIX RISES

A.J. Moorling was once a brilliant writer, creating a phenomenon in the early twenty-first century with her *Henry Popper* series. She's lived a long life, but at the ripe age of one-hundred and nine and three-quarters, she's decided it's her time to travel on.

As I sit with her inside the parlor of her country home—one of a few still in existence, with the popping up of megacities across the globe, and the excessive desertification that followed—I can't help but notice how young her blue eyes appear, almost childlike.

Bright orbs float into position and shoot on, bathing the room in radiant white light. Eduardo, the technician, is one of the best in the industry. His holoforms are so realistic and detailed that you'd swear they have mass. He adjusts the globes with the fiber optic-glove on his left hand, until the room is set. With a final light scan, freezing the image of Ms. Moorling and her lap dog, Sergeant Popper, the diagnostics are completed.

We are ready to begin.

Surveillance bugs flit throughout the room, sending unique images back to Roy Vargas, the production manager at Studio C, in Tianshi, formerly Los Angeles, California.

"All set," Roy's voice booms from my ear pod.

"Go on sound," Eduardo says.

Ms. Moorling pets her Shi Tzu, who sits like a hideous gargoyle in her lap.

I lean closer. "He's just lovely."

"Yes," Ms. Moorling says, a smile crossing her cracked lips. "He's been with me through it all, actually inspired the entire Henry Popper series. He's the one you should be interviewing."

I laugh, knowing the cameras are rolling. Even though the interview hasn't started, the mechanical insects hovering all around us already capture every nuance through glowing-red eyes.

"How old *is* he?" I ask.

"Eighty-six, this spring."

"In dog years?"

"No, people years. I'd had his DNA frozen in the 20's for cloning. This is the fourth generation of Sergeant Popper, you see?"

I nod, now grasping the sizeable fortune Ms. Moorling has acquired in her lifetime. The cost to clone an animal is an exorbitant amount, but to have it done four times is unfathomable.

"We're ready, Cathy."

I snap back. Eduardo is motioning it's a go. Makeup artists bounce up for a final powder, and the room falls silent.

With the notoriety of Ms. Moorling, and the fact that this is her final interview, I know the whole world will be watching. *Henry Popper* has been translated into every known language, including a mathematical adaptation, for any future contact with aliens.

Sweat beads beneath the powder layered on my brow, the lights as hot as the basement of Gnoblers Bank from book three. I am suddenly sticking to my seat. Heart racing, I listen to Eduardo's countdown: camera one…roll on sound…speed…marker…

Pointing at me, his fingers mark five….

Four…

Ms. Moorling strokes her dog's fur.

Three…

Can the entire planet hear my hammering heart?

Two…

"Good evening, and welcome to Tianshi Nightly's exclusive, one-on-one with the distinguished lady herself, A.J. Moorling."

"You're too kind," Ms. Moorling says, turning on her charm.

"Ms. Moorling, I'll get right to it. I'm told this is to be your final interview."

"Yes, I'm afraid so." She pets Sergeant Popper, who is now snoring softly in her lap. "It's just my time, dear. I've lived longer than I should have, thanks to modern science, but—I'm tired now."

I feel my forehead scrunch through the caked powder cemented by sweat. "Are you ill?"

Ms. Moorling laughs. "No, dear. People of my stature can afford the luxury of avoiding sickness."

"Are you dying?"

"Only by choice. You see, when Henry Popper touched the lives of so many children over seventy years ago, I wanted to live forever, to watch the joy fill the faces of new children each year as they were exposed to Henry Popper's adventures for the first time."

The dog's ears twitch. Mechanical bugs swarm, hanging on her every word. Claustrophobia weighs heavy on my shoulders. I fight myself to remain seated.

"But over time," she continues, "I've seen, to my own sheer heartache, that kids don't read anymore. Not like they used to. And really, why should they? With holofilms and self-directed gaming...a writer using mere words, such as myself, cannot compete. I get swept beneath the rug of technology."

"I see," I say, using my most sympathetic voice. "Why not create a more competitive product using this technology, to reach those children unfamiliar with your stories?"

She laughs. "I'm an old woman, and I still believe in the power of the imagination. It has the strength to create worlds or destroy them, to move mountains or climb them. Technology will never replace imagination. And it's the only place these bloody bugs have yet to infiltrate." She points at the surveillance surrounding us.

"Yet," I reiterate.

She gives me a nasty look, to which I reply with my sweetest smile. That should translate nicely on camera. Ms. Moorling quickly recovers, returning a sugar-coated grin of her own. After all, the whole world is watching.

"So, what's next for the great A.J. Moorling?" I announce.

She flashes a wry smile. "What else? The-End."

A fireball erupts from her paisley chair, engulfing Ms. Moorling and Sergeant Popper in a flare of bluish-orange flames.

I jump back, out of my seat.

Eduardo is shouting commands.

The crew is in action, running around the room, looking for water to douse the fire.

Someone yanks me from behind.

The mechanical bugs zoom in and out, catching every second of the mayhem, at every possible angle.

And just like that, it stops.

Ashes fill the paisley chair. From beneath them, the charred corner of a box juts up through the shimmering black dust. I reach for it, surprised to find it isn't hot. "There's something inside."

"Well, open it," Roy commands in my ear.

I can almost see the lust in his eyes as he drools over the ratings this broadcast will bring him. The fluttering camera-bugs are so close I can feel them brush across my skin, through my hair, embedding into my eardrums to access my thoughts. It's strange to me, how A.J. Moorling has disappeared, probably forever, and no one seems upset.

Am I even upset?

All these years of suppressing emotions, and keeping my feelings hidden from the constant onslaught of cameras.

Living behind a mask I've imagined into existence.

Never knowing which of my actions are caught on camera or who is reviewing the feed.

We've become a society devoid of feeling.

A tear trails down my cheek. I can't stop it, but I don't care that the whole world is watching. Opening the box, I gasp audibly.

The Phoenix Rises:
the final book in the Henry Popper series

And it hits me.

This was all a scam, a front to launch a new book. A real book, that kids can hold in their hands with pages they can manually turn. And what a way to catch the eyes and ears of the world then by having her final book rise from her ashes.

Brilliant.

Facing the cameras, I wipe away my tear. "I don't know what has become of A.J. Moorling, but I hope she has found peace. Her legacy is here with us in the final installment of her life's work. The last book she ever wrote, from the first story she ever created."

The orbs extinguish, taking away the plastic look from the room, revealing the true colors and textures around me. They are flawed in this light. Unnatural, uneven. But they are real, something I have forgotten.

I open the book to the first page, where a handwritten message is scribed:

Dear Cathy,

I know you'll understand one day, when you're my age, why I did what I did. Living in a world devoid of true emotions is no place for a writer to live at all. Or any human being, for that matter.

Thank you for the opportunity to share my final words.

Your friend,
A.J. Moorling

ZOMBIE TURKEY
A THANKSGIVING TALE OF TERROR

"Thank you for calling the Butterorb Turkey hotline. What is your emergency?"

"Yeah, hey…Gosh, I can't believe someone really answered. I thought this was a prank number. You know, to a joke store or a body shop or—"

"Sir," I interrupt. "What is your emergency?"

All I hear is dead air. He's hung up.

Wouldn't be the first time someone called just verifying the number is real. Yes, I work at the call center for Butterorb Turkey. Don't laugh. It's a real job. For the month of November, I answer all sorts of phone calls on the basting and frying, smoking and brining of turkeys. I share recipes, I help explain the importance of cooking the proper pounds per hour, and I've been there for more people than I'd care to admit, who have called with smoke pouring out of their oven because their turkey is on fire.

I'd guestimate about half the country has take-out Chinese or pizza on Thanksgiving Day; especially on a year like this one, when a horrible bird flu wiped out a majority of the poultry in the country in late October.

So here I am, manning the phone lines on the 3-6

am shift—seniority has its privileges—when my phone rings. I flip the switch and take the call. "Thank you for calling the Butterorb Turkey hotline. What is your emergency?"

"You gotta help me," a man shouts.

I lean forward in my seat. "Calm down, sir."

"Oh my God. Help me."

"Sir, what seems to be the problem?"

"She's trying to kill me."

A fresh chill sweeps down my spine, which is not because the room is as cold as a freezer. "If someone is trying to kill you, sir, you need to hang up and dial 9-1-1."

The excitement in my voice evokes some rubbernecking by a few coworkers.

"Not someone," the man says. "Some *thing*."

I hear glass breaking in the background from wherever the man is calling from. "I'm sorry, sir. Did you say some *thing* is trying to kill you?"

"Yes! That's exactly what I said. Please, help me."

I flip my light from green to red, indicating to my floor supervisor the severity of the call, although I'm still not sure what I'm dealing with. I listen in on the phone calls my coworkers have taken: Over salting the turkey? An easy fix. Smoke a sixteen pound turkey for how many hours? Child's play. I wonder how I got the crazy caller, whose probably pulling my leg—or drumstick, as we like to say around here.

"I really don't believe I'm qualified to help you, sir."

"Are you freaking kidding me?"

His raspy breaths lead me to believe he's running.

"You are the Butterorb people, aren't you?" he

asks.

"Yes, sir. America's finest turkey."

"Then this is your problem."

My supervisor scoots closer.

"What did you say was trying to kill you?"

"A turkey," he says. "A Butterorb turkey."

Everything stops for a minute and all I hear is silence. My supervisor's lips are moving, but it takes a few seconds for her voice to catch up to my ears. "Penny," she says. "Take the call."

I shake my head clear. "That's not possible, sir. Our turkeys are farm raised and stay on that farm until shipment—"

"Not a live turkey. It's the one I bought for Thanksgiving."

I grab ahold of my headset, as if that will clarify what I just heard. "Wait a minute. Are you trying to tell me that your Thanksgiving turkey…is trying to kill you?"

"Yes! That's what I've been saying."

I frantically type shorthand codes into my computer. "Well that is our problem."

"You're telling me."

"What's your name, sir?"

"Ole McDonald."

"Seriously?"

"Seriously. My mother was Swedish."

"Okay. Weight?"

"Around two-twenty-five."

"Not you, the turkey."

"Oh. She's a twenty-six pounder."

As I type, sweat slips like melting butter down my temples. "Head or no head?"

"Headless."

"Hmm, and I thought only chickens could do that." I pause. "Mr. McDonald, what makes you think she's trying to kill you?"

"Oh, I don't know…because she's chasing me with my battery-powered carving knife!"

The room starts spinning. What can I do? After seventeen Thanksgivings, I've never dealt with anything like this before. Our turkeys are shipped from the farm to this very building where I sit. They are processed and packaged with great care. Unlike some chicken outfits, we ate the loss of our turkeys that became infected by the bird flu. They are in containment and waiting incineration. It will smell good when they go up, but those turkeys are not edible.

"On behalf of Butterorb," I say, "let me apologize for the inconvenience our turkey may have caused you."

"Inconvenience? Lady, an inconvenience would be if the little red button never popped, and I overcooked Thanksgiving dinner."

I blink, shake my head, and find my second wind. "You're so right. Where are you right now?"

"Hiding in my closet."

"I'm going to help you, but I need you to help me too."

"Okay. Shoot."

"Since there's no explanation for this…walking dead turkey, I'll need the bar code on the packaging."

"But that's all the way in the kitchen." McDonald's panic has somehow risen.

"Perfect. Because I also think I know how to really

kill this turkey."

"How?"

"You've got to get her in the broiler. A quick, hot oven may be just what you need to cook her goose."

"Turkey."

"Whatever. On three, I want you to get to the kitchen as quickly as possible, and find that shrink wrap. The faster I get those numbers, the sooner we'll know what we're dealing with."

"Okay. I'll try."

"Good. One…two…three."

I listen as Ole McDonald lets out a primal scream while sprinting to his kitchen. I imagine him zipping through halls lined with family portraits, and taking his apartment's stairs two at a time. Then again, he could live on a farm.

"I'm in the kitchen," McDonald says, panting. "No sign of her."

"Great. Crank the broiler to high."

"Done."

"You're doing fine, Mr. McDonald. Now, I need you to find the wrapping."

"Okay."

I hear him sift through his garbage can.

"Found it."

"Perfect. I need you to read the six-digit number at the bottom."

"Okay. One-one-two-eight-She's coming!"

"Mr. McDonald? Ole?"

He's screaming, running again. I type in the numbers he's given so far. Fifteen hundred shipments start with this set. Suddenly, everything goes quiet. My mouth is dry. "Mr. McDonald?" I crack. "Ole?"

"I'm here," he whispers. "I'm in the utility room."

"Where's the turkey?"

"I don't know."

He's crying, panicked.

"Oh, God. She's gonna kill me! She's…Oh, God. She'll eat me alive."

Between his sobs, I say, "You're gonna be okay. I'm here with you now. I promise, nothing will happen."

He's calming, sniffling.

"Ole, I need the rest of the numbers. Can you do that? Can you read them to me?"

"I don't know. It's dark in here."

"Is your washer-dryer in there?"

"Yes."

"Open the dryer. There should be a light inside."

I hear the metal pop, and then squeal on rusty hinges. "Got it. One-one-two-eight-one-three."

"You're doing amazing, Mr. McDonald."

I type in the remaining digits, noticing for the first time that the whole room has quieted. Every attendant is chewing their cuticles hanging on each word of my conversation, which is fed through the PA system to each headset. I wait for the numbers to find a match, and freeze like a shipped turkey when they do.

11-28-13, the code placed on the batch of fowl testing positive for the bird flu.

"Oh my God." Slowly, I stand.

"What is it?"

Turkeys, hundreds of turkeys, are running the length of the halls surrounding control center. Their feathered bodies reach past window level as they charge toward the door.

A tear rolls down my cheek.

"Mr. McDonald, your turkey has been infected by the Z-2013 bird flu, a highly contagious, and once believed to be deadly, fowl virus."

"What are you talking about?"

The turkeys are cracking the glass with their beaks and claws, their heads still intact.

"Sir, if you come into contact with your turkey—"

"She's at the door. Oh, God. She's breaking it down."

Turkeys flood into the control station, decaying flesh and rotting feathers dripping off like too much breading.

"She's in the room!"

I hear the electric blade mixed with Mr. McDonald's screams until the call is dropped and the phones goes dead. Like Ole, I'm sure.

The bird flu must have interacted with the turkeys on a cellular level, infecting them like a cancer, and bringing them back from the dead. Well, mostly dead. But unlike Ole McDonald, the turkeys hunting here still have their heads and beaks.

And they're eating people.

I run for as long as I can before I'm swarmed by the zombie turkeys, carving me like I have their kind for so many years. I guess it's only fair that they take their revenge. But my heart goes out to the millions stuffing tur-duck-hens this holiday season who will be in for a triple-homicidal disaster on more than one level.

I almost took a job opening at the post office handling letters for Santa, but with the potential for mail bombs, I declined, afraid I could die. Who'd have thought working in a turkey call center would be my demise. The turkeys did.

And they're not finished.

This Thanksgiving Day, people may not be eating turkey. The turkeys may be eating them.

THE FALCON

Sokoloff knew he had a problem when the Rover started spitting out nothing but rock. He stepped out of the cab, crawling along the grate to the front grill of the massive sixteen metric ton machine and opened the engine panel. No steam. No sparks. No flames. That was good. Compressing the node behind his left ear, Sokoloff said, "Computer, full diagnostic on Rover, bravo one-two-three-sixty."

The computer transmitted data over the chip embedded beneath his skin, which was processed and displayed on the 3-D screen before his left eye.

"Great," he said. "Cylinder's blown. That'll take all day."

In the distance, a towering wall of black clouds rolled closer. Lightning exploded in brilliant red and gold flashes. Sokoloff realized he didn't have all day. He returned to the Rover's cab and swiped a comm screen onto the dash. A blonde android appeared onscreen, wearing a navy blue coverall and cap donning the Polzin Industries emblem. She was the next generation of FALCON, or Flexible Automaton Link-Controlled Offline Nanobots, the innovation that put Polzin on the map. A pioneering program of AI androids that could navigate nanobots without any human assistance; and like the ancient Egyptian hieroglyphs depicted Falcons as gods, these robotic *gods* controlled most of the operations on the Mars base.

"FALCON, the Rover's bad. Probably got some Mars dust in the gears and blew a cylinder."

"Sending Ana," she replied, before the screen disappeared.

Near the end of the 21st century, uranium sources neared depletion on Earth. Polzin Industries, in conjunction with the UN, sent cosmonauts to Mars to mine marsconium, a clean consumable energy source found deep in the planet's core. Sokoloff had immediately volunteered to oversee the FALCONs operations. He and his crew had stayed on the transport ship for several months while nanobots built an enviro-dome 150 kilometers high covering over 90 kilometers of Mars's red surface.

With a manufactured environment similar to Earth's, the cosmonauts could work within the dome without the bulk of spacesuits and helmets. Mining was the same here as it was on Earth, tedious, dangerous, and requiring split-second decisions and maneuvering capabilities, which meant the difference between life and death. Only a few months into the mission, a marsconium deposit was discovered hundreds of meters deep. And after three years, Sokoloff was still mining that find.

But at night, when it was quiet, Sokoloff thought of Milana.

While he waited for the repair module, Sokoloff sat back in the Rover's pilot seat and took out a flask.

He gulped a hot mouthful of the spirits and grimaced. Alcohol on the Mars base was illegal, but the same machinery used to distill his water worked fine to make his drink.

After half an hour, Ana rolled up churning red dust behind her. Rock crunched beneath the tread of her tank wheels as she approached and parked. A highly advanced nanobot's repair system, Ana could do things and get in places that no human being ever could. Sokoloff put away his flask and got back to work.

"Hello, baby." He opened Ana's hatch and pulled out a length of tubing. Pressing the node behind his ear again, he said, "FALCON, initialize diagnostics and repairs on Rover, bravo one-two-three-sixty."

"Initializing."

Hundreds of thousands of flea-sized robots burst from the tubing and attached to the Rover performing diagnostic checks. The information was relayed between them in a millionth of a second as the nanobots worked with the precision and unity of an army of ants.

"Rover clear," announced the FALCON. "Checking shaft."

Moving as one living organism, the nanobots sped down the 800 meter shaft to check the rest of the Rover's components.

Sokoloff watched as the raging storm beat on the curved walls of the dome. In three years, he had never seen a storm this fierce. Luckily, he was the only human left on this rock, unless you counted humanoid robots. The storm season on Mars lasted six weeks, with a replacement crew due to arrive at the season's

end, less than a week away. Although he was
petitioned to evacuate, Sokoloff refused to abandon
Ana.

Not like he had Milana.

The dome shook violently. Something wasn't
right. Sokoloff rushed back to the Rover's cab and
cued up the comm screen. "What's going on?" he
asked the FALCON. He'd forget she was an android
sometimes, her anthropomimetic features set in perfect
proportion.

"Electromagnetic storm. Category eleven.
Sustained winds at four hundred and sixty kilometers."

"Are you sure?"

"I have not been programmed with opinions."

Sokoloff ran his fingers through his black hair.
Lightning strobed above the dome spindling down the
curved lens like fire-rain.

"Probability of dome survival, eighteen percent."

"Eighteen percent? That can't be right. Get a
message to Dr. Polzin that—"

"Communication with Earth is not possible.
Advise immediate return to the ship."

Sokoloff shook his head. "I can't do that. Ana's
down the shaft."

"Survival probability dropping eleven point two
percent every minute. Ana's survival probability
remains at one-hundred percent."

Sokoloff swore under his breath as he jumped into
the cab of the rover. He turned over the engine and
forced the gears into place. As he drove away, he saw
a flicker of Milana's face and he swore he saw one of
the nanobots shoot out of the shaft. Ana wanted his
attention. She didn't want him to go.

He jammed on the brakes.

"I'm not leaving her," he said through gritted teeth, then slid the holographic screen across the dash until the FALCON disappeared.

Sokoloff jumped out of the rover and ran back toward the shaft. The dome rattled as an above ground earthquake, until with a deafening crack, a weak joint in the dome collapsed, then tore open. The wind flooded in the fissure at an alarming rate. Sokoloff's pulse raced even faster. He dove into the back of the Rover and strapped on an oxygen mask. The doors hissed closed, sealing him in and he grabbed the emergency suit from the rear, quickly stripping down to his undergarments to put it on. The tight reflective suit fit like a second skin. The Rover suddenly rattled. Sokoloff looked out the window.

"Oh, my God."

The dome peeled back and scrolled at the edges.

Ana was still out there.

Sokoloff put on his helmet. He switched the comm link to manual using the buttons on the forearm of his suit. "FALCON," he said. "Send Ana up."

"Negative," the FALCON replied. "Diagnostics are not complete."

A chill stopped Sokoloff dead in his tracks. Ana had never disregarded his commands before. Shuffling back into the cab, he shouted, "Abort! Abort! Send Ana up, now!"

Lightning sliced through the air with a crack. Blinding light filled Sokoloff's visor. The hairs on the back of his neck stood on end. Reaching for the door panel, he repeated, "Abort diagnostics!"

"No."

No? How could that be possible? "Did you say, 'no'?" Sokoloff asked, dumbfounded.

"Diagnostics are seventy-three percent complete. Abort impossible."

Sokoloff's body tingled as the color drained from his face. What was happening? Why was the FALCON not taking orders? Had its programming been fried?

The storm.

The electromagnetism of the Mars lightning must be disturbing the android's inner workings, rebooting her. He would need to override the system manually, which meant he had to go out in the storm. He had to get to Ana. He couldn't leave her to be destroyed by something outside her control.

Not like he had Milana.

He slid open the cab door, his boots skidding across the steel grate, and pressed through the blinding copper dust toward the mobile mainframe encased in a steel cage several yards away.

Milana had been six years old when the cancer hit. He had prayed, begging God to take him instead of his little girl. When God didn't cure her, Sokoloff had worked for a cure of his own, finding a way to get nanobots into his daughter's bloodstream to attack and destroy the cancer cells. Millions of nanobots acting as little gods were mixed with his own DNA to make the autonomous robots organic, allowing the biomimetrics to pick up where her own blood cells had failed. Ana.

He and Ana would fight the cancer with her.

Reaching the mainframe, he forced the steel doors open, and punched in abort codes on the panel to stop the FALCON and save Ana.

"Stop!" the FALCON fired through his headset. "Stop!"

Somehow when Ana had been inside of Milana, Milana's DNA had merged with the nanobots, and although Ana hadn't succeeded, and Milana had succumbed to the cancer, a piece of her still lived inside Ana's core. Tears slipped down Sokoloff's cheeks.

He could still save her.

The thunderous quake proceeded the swarm of nanobots funneling up the shaft and out onto the surface like hungry locusts. As one, they charged Sokoloff, knocking him to his back and blanketing his suit, tearing away at the pliable metal shrouding his body, and invading his helmet to embed into his skin. One by one, Ana ate through his flesh, devouring his muscles to enter his bloodstream; millions of machines moving under the FALCON's command.

He remembered Milana's face before she became sick, that summer at the beach house when they held hands and played in the surf. The sun glinted off her blonde hair, the same shade as her mother's. He'd postponed his trip to Mars when Milana got sick, and he'd told her many stories about the Red Planet.

"Daddy, will you take me to Mars someday?"

If she only knew.

Her laughter echoed in his ears, as Ana consumed his whole being, the FALCON infiltrating his body and mind, fully controlling him.

"I love you, daddy," Milana had said, holding him tight. "Promise me we'll be together forever."

And as Sokoloff heard the FALCON say, "Diagnostics complete," his body no longer under his control, his soul permanently imprisoned behind his mind, he could finally fulfill his promise to his daughter.

They *would* be together forever.

JUST PASSING THROUGH

"Sometimes, when it's quiet, I remember what my life was like before moving to Cedar Springs."

I spoke to the balding bartender wearing a name tag that read *Bill* who acted like he couldn't hear me as he dried glasses then slid them in the rack above his head without a word. A half-filled glass of brandy sat before me. "At first, it was strange being here. Took some getting used to. All the rules were different and nothing made much sense."

Bill turned to grab more glasses from the rack.

"True story," I said. "I walked up to this woman once in the parlor sipping tea and I said, "Looks like rain." Well, you'da think she'd seen a ghost, the way she up and ran outta the room, knocking her tea cup to the ground where it shattered. I tried picking up the pieces, but I couldn't. Just had to watch it all slip through my fingers."

Bill looked up with an uninterested smile.

"I used to be a pilot back in North Carolina after The Great War," I bragged. "I flew people around; rich folk, who could afford the solo flight just for the fun of it."

Bill walked to the end of the bar to wait on a new patron. I didn't mind. I just kept on going with my story. Not like Bill was really listening anyway. "Then, I moved here. Was just passing through at first, but after a while the old house grew on me. Some say it's like early retirement. I don't know. I feel too young to be retired."

"But she did see a ghost, din't she?"

"Excuse me?" I turned and saw a colored man standing behind me.

"Da woman. Dat's what spooked her, ain't it?"

I shrugged at the newbie. I didn't have a particular fondness for newbies.

"It seems lotsa folks dat comes here is looking to see a ghost." The fellow took a seat beside me, eyes darting around like he's been followed. "I can't tell 'em apart, most times. The folks here to visit and the ones dats been moved here."

"It takes some time." I reached for the glass of brandy and pretended to take a sip. "The folks that are here to stay don't usually carry any luggage."

The fellow slapped his thigh. "Dat's it. You hit da nail on da head."

His hearty laugh took me back to my life before Cedar Springs. I remember laughing a lot more then. With a loud creak, the swing door leading to the kitchen flew open and a large man wearing a trench coat stood in the entranceway. In his hand, some sort of a machine the size of a brick beeped and ticked causing an awful lot of ruckus that seemed to get louder the closer he came.

"We'd better move," I told the fellow next to me.

"Why's dat?"

"Cause of that man over there."

"What's wrong with him?"

"Follow me. He won't bother you if you don't bother him."

We left the bar quickly passing the man who seemed not to notice us, busying himself with running his beeping contraption along the walls and trim.

"What's your name?" I asked the fellow as we settled in the parlor.

"Crevis. Crevis Jones." He extended a hand which I ignored. Crevis lowered it along with his eyes.

"I'm Bryce Morgan Longfellow, the third," I told him, pretending to smoke a cigar someone left smoldering in the ashtray.

"Why do you do that?"

"Do what?" I asked.

"Act like you're smokin' and drinkin', but not act'lly doin' it."

I sighed. "Old habits die hard, Crevis. Found a lot of things I did in my old life I just can't do here in Cedar Springs, new rules and all."

A tabby strolled into the parlor. Crevis reached out to pet it. "Here kitty, kitty."

The cat hissed; its hair sticking out in so many directions it looked like it had been shocked full of electricity. I belly laughed as Crevis recoiled his hand and scooted his legs up underneath him.

"What's wrong with dat cat?" Crevis asked.

"He doesn't like newbies."

Crevis worked to catch his breath. "Coulda warned me, ya know?"

"Where's the fun in that?" I said with a smile.

The man with the equipment entered the parlor. I stood, motioning for Crevis to follow me up the squeaking staircase to my bedroom. It had a small sitting area near the fireplace where Crevis and I took a seat.

"Nice room," Crevis said. "How long you been here?"

"Fifty-three years," I said, staring toward the window.

"Woohee. Dat's a long time, ain't it?"

"Sure is," I said, picking at my nails.

Crevis shook his head. "Not me. No siree. I'm jus' passin' through. I never stay put in the same place for too long."

"Whatever you say," I said, stepping over to the window. Beneath the oaks and maples blocking my view, a wide lake spanned the length of the vast property. Surrounding it, manicured flower beds, budded in every shade of the rainbow, gently waved in the light breeze.

Crevis stood and joined me. About twenty or thirty people dressed in garments from many different eras walked the grounds: A woman in a plush Victorian. A boy wearing knickers and tights. A gentleman dressed in a topcoat and hat. A young girl draped in a flapper dress too big for her tiny frame.

"Why dey dressed dat way?" Crevis asked, pointing.

"There's all kinds here, Crevis. Most find that they have no reason to leave after a while."

Crevis faced me. "And what about you? Are you one of dem?"

I smiled. "Yes. We all are sooner or later." I

moved away from the window back to my seat. Crossing my leg and adjusting the cuff of my trousers, I said, "Even you, Crevis."

His face would've reddened, if circumstances had been different. "Me? Nah, I'm afraid you've got me all wrong, boss."

I stared at Crevis. This was my favorite part. "What's the last thing you remember, Crevis? Before you came to Cedar Springs?"

Crevis's forehead crinkled and he thought a long while before he answered. "I was walkin' down the street back home, jus' mindin' my own business. Outta nowhere, dis man shows up wearing a dark cloak like he was from someplace else and ain't never been dere before. He don't say nothin' 'tal, jus' stared at me real serious-like. Then, a second man comes running 'round da corner, waving a gun in the air, cussin' and screamin'. I jus' turn real fast and starts runnin', when I hear a loud pop, like his gun goin' off. Next thing I know, I'm on the doorstep here in Cedar Springs."

My smile widened. "And did you come with or without luggage?"

Crevis wiped his forehead out of instinct, the stress rising up in him like a summertime thermometer. "Without. But I don't remember ever comin' here before. Or never wantin' to come here neither."

"No one ever does."

Crevis's voice rose in panic. "What is dis place, Mr. Longfella?"

"I thought you'd never ask." I stood, spreading my arms out to indicate our surroundings. "This is the Bailey House of Cedar Springs, Michigan."

Crevis looked puzzled. "The Bailey House? But

dat dere's a haunted house."

I nodded. "And you are its newest resident."

Crevis stared at me, just blinking real fast.

"Crevis? You all right?" I asked.

He just kept blinking. Finally, he said, "So, I'm a...ghost?"

"That's right," I told him. "Just like the rest of us."

Crevis began to laugh. He laughed so hard that I bet he would've been crying if he still had tears in his tear ducts. "You crazy!" he shouted through his rifts. "You about the craziest man I ever met."

The door slid open. It was the man with the machine.

"Oh, really?" I said, pointing. "Then why don't you go and talk to him."

"Okay. I will."

Crevis stomped up to the man and stood right in his face. The man didn't seem to notice. I covered my laugh with my hand.

"Excuse me, sir?" Crevis said. There was no response. Crevis cleared his throat. "Sir? Excuse me?"

Laughing aloud, I suggested, "Maybe you ought to say it louder. Perhaps he's hard of hearing."

Shouting, Crevis said, "EXCUSE ME, SIR!"

The man's eyes bulged as he caught a glimpse of Crevis. I've found that once the wall is broken down, the visitors can see us all. Turning to face me, I smiled at the man and said very gentlemanlike, "Boo."

The man screamed as he tripped over himself to clear out of the room then took a tumble down the stairs before landing hard in the foyer. He didn't even shut the front door when he ran out.

I was doubled-over laughing so hard it should

have hurt. The look on Crevis's face was pure confusion.

"What was that all about?" Crevis asked.

I stood upright, placing an arm around Crevis's shoulder. "They come here to find a ghost, but I don't think they ever really expect to see one."

Crevis started to wobble a bit. "Woah, Crevis." I reached out to brace him with my other arm. "Why you're as white as a ghost."

"You're not funny, boss," he said, as I helped him over to a chair.

"It's all I got left, Crevis, my sense of humor. The rest of me was trampled by a horse and buried six-feet under."

Crevis looked up at me. "You serious, aintchya?"

I nodded slowly.

"So, now what?"

I shrugged. "Well, seeing as how you didn't bring any luggage to unpack how about I show you around and introduce you to everyone. 'Cause you may be here a while."

"That's a mighty fine, idea, Mr. Longfella. Mighty fine."

"Please, Crevis. Call me Bryce."

As we climbed downstairs, the front door opened. A woman in a tattered dress stood on the porch holding hands with a little girl not more than five-years-old. And the first thing I noticed was that neither one of them was carrying any luggage.

THE HEIST

Edwin Black spotted him the moment he stepped off the train. The balding man wiped condensation off his red-tinted oval glasses as he scanned the crowd. His trophy bride—junior to him by nearly twenty years—descended the steps. Her low cut leather gown and corset presented her ample bosom, her hands covered in matching leather kid gloves. Following close behind a broad, heavyset woman cradled a six month old baby. Edwin's gaze stopped upon the baby.

The husband and wife waved and flashed smiles to the gathered crowd as they made their way to the opened door of their Crane Model 3. They climbed into the cabin and settled in. The baby fussed briefly. The driver squeezed the horn as the steam engine hissed and sprayed rolling the vehicle's thin wheels out of the station.

Edwin flipped open his pocket watch and studied the encased photo on the underside of the bronze lid among the bits and pieces of gears from his travels down the US East Coast soldered inside the watch face. He imagined the fair woman's blue eyes and red hair filtered through the grainy print. It had been her idea to adopt the baby girl to the wealthy couple, after learning that the trophy bride was barren. A large sum of money was discussed and the coal baron's wife had been happy to oblige. Hunger pangs will do that to you. Now phase two was underway, and Edwin imagined no one would see it coming.

He strolled down Duval Street toward Stewart's Hall. Synthesized keys hammered music through the opened door of the bar before Edwin even rounded the block corner. He pushed through the crowd to an empty seat at the bar. The bartender took a tankard of distilled spirits and poured him a shot, waited for Edwin to swallow it, then poured another, before returning the pewter container to the mélange of bronze slats, corded pewter pegs, and wrought iron fasteners connected as modernized shelves before mirrored panes. He stepped back to the far end of the glazed countertop beneath which a junkyard of relics lay sprawled out to the two men who Edwin recognized. The one had black hair with a manicured beard like vines; the other painted with bronze makeup matching his beaver vest and polished fingernails. They sat around a third man Edwin pinned as a newcomer.

"Find the queen," the bartender said, sliding three facedown cards so quickly their pattern blurred.

The newcomer's silk shirt was a patchwork of sweat. A small mountain of cash sat off to his side. He carefully hovered a long-nailed index finger back and forth over the cards, finally pointing hard to one. The bartender flipped a jack. The man brought both hands to his head pulling his slicked back hair out to the sides in wild spikes as the bartender raked the newcomer's cash away from of him, his white belled shirt ends trailing like the gaping mouth of a toothless fish. With a slur of profanities, the newcomer placed his black coachman's hat askew, finished his drink, and stormed out. The bartender laughed.

"You sure were lucky, Teddy," said the man with the pruned beard. "You've been on a roll tonight."

"Luck don't have nothin' to do with it," the bartender said. "You just gotta know what cards you're dealt before you go tryin' to beat the odds."

Edwin sipped his spirits as the bartender picked up the three cards. Edwin smirked. All of them were jacks.

After several drinks Edwin settled his tab and left downtown's imperial light district. The long walk was cool and quiet, the darkness and chirping crickets his only companions, besides the distant burping of factory pipes billowing smoke into the humid smog of industry he'd left behind. A nearly full moon's light struggled through the trees casting spotted pools of white across Edwin's path.

He had strolled along this path many times in the past few weeks, taking surveillance of the mansion while the couple was away. It was perfect really, the modern home much more secluded than their home in the country. If only the trophy bride had understood. She could have considered someone else's baby instead of laying hold of this one. But the pain of leaving the coal tycoon without a seed to carry on his legacy must have been too strong for her to bear, and her love for him, Edwin imagined, had clouded her judgment.

Edwin stared up at the pale, bluish moon, thinking of the eyes of the woman in the picture, eyes warm and redolent of love past. He thought of her red ringlets lying across her forehead, the softness of her buttermilk skin, and her laugh, both familiar and long-forgotten.

Night fell like a heavy cloak as he reached the polished silver walls of the sleek, angular mansion, the lamps long retired. Without missing a beat Edwin skated through the shadows, down the cobblestone drive, and to the front doors. He removed his lock picks and got to work, the lock mechanism like gears of a clock. With a soft click, the lock gave way and the front door slid open on the gears and cogs allowing Edwin entrance into the metallic mansion. The door closed behind him. The steady ticking of the brass streamlined Victorian timepiece met him as a doorman.

He scanned the floral papered walls of the foyer, appreciating the wielded brass cabinets and in the great room beyond, the Victorian settee couches with blood red cushions inlaid across a steel frame. Edwin moved about, confident the coast was clear from the heavy snores drifting down from the master bedroom. He reached the stairway, stopping short with one foot on the bottom step. Someone was there with him. The clock ticked loudly. His hands dampened with sweat. He jumped when the family's cat rubbed against his legs, stalking with a purr. Relieved, Edwin continued his climb.

At the top, a quiet had come over the home, the faint snores suddenly silenced. Edwin kept his breath locked in his lungs. Then, after a soft choking noise, like a throat being cleared, the snoring continued, and Edwin exhaled relief.

He scuttled down the hall, passed an open door where the deep snores from the nurse maid rumbled out, and stopped before a closed door with a spiraling wrought iron knob. He reached out and turned it slowly. It opened on well-oiled hinges, the door pulled back by its steel cable, revealing a large nursery with pale pink walls bordered with dancing ballerina wallpaper. Porcelain dolls and wooden toys sat patiently in the corner awaiting the growing baby's hands that would never touch them.

The cradle sat beneath a canopy of chiffon in the center of the room. Edwin slid the cloth aside and gazed at the sleeping child. Her hair was strawberry blonde and curled into small ringlets, her skin the same milky-white shade as her mother's. Gently, he lifted the baby into his arms. She fussed, but found solace nuzzled in the crook of Edwin's neck. He shimmied back down the hall then carefully down the stairway, where the grinding cogs of the clock met him again, though this time the chiming hour gave Edwin the fleeting and ridiculous thought it had done so to give him away.

He hurried out the front door concentrating on escape while keeping the baby still. Focused on his breathing, he trotted through the courtyard and down the cobblestone drive. He prayed the couple and their nursemaid would not wake up before he reached the rendezvous point.

Edwin crossed the long driveway and reached the main street turning up it as the baby, now awake and wailing, bounced in his arms. Hidden beneath the boughs of a large oak tree sat the waiting vehicle, steam pouring out in rifts from the exhaust. The exposed engine swept back on steel beams, the black canvas roof pushed down in the back. Edwin came to a stop outside the passenger door.

"Give her to me," said the redhead from the photo reaching up hungry arms.

Edwin handed the baby to her mother.

"Hello, little one," the redhead cooed. She embraced the baby girl, breathed in her scent, and kissed her head. With an unfeigned smile, Edwin pushed the car quietly toward town feeling the filigreed detailed wood paneling beneath his fingertips.

The woman turned and said, "I can't believe we did it."

"Don't celebrate yet," he replied. "We still have to reach port, which could be swarming with police officers if they discover the baby is gone before we ship out."

Her blue eyes widened. "Did anyone hear you?"

"Not a chance," he said. "But that doesn't mean things can't still go wrong."

The woman gave the baby a bottle, then looked over her shoulder at Edwin. "I don't ever want to do anything like this again."

"Come now. Do you think I would let anything happen to my girl?" He charmed her with his dimpled smile and she was pacified. "Besides, getting all that money from those two rich fools will float us for a long time. Their little obsession with appearances outweighed their common good senses."

"I'm sure you're right, but no more heists using our baby," she snapped. "You ask me, I think we just got lucky."

"Luck doesn't have anything to do with it," Edwin

said. "You just have to know the cards you're dealt." He looked over his shoulder, then back to the road. "And right now, we could use a good hand."

"Why's that?" she asked, looking at the baby.

"Because there's an upstairs lamp burning in the mansion."

Without need to remain quiet, Edwin hopped behind the steering wheel, cranked the heat beneath the closed loop water tank, and rushed it across the condenser. Steam poured through the turbines pitching the car forward with a clunk of welded metal and brass fixtures.

"Sure hope we make it to port," Edwin said, "before the couple realizes the baby they bought has been taken back."

"And what if we don't?"

Edwin shrugged. "It's the price we pay for bluffing a game with only jacks."

FARFROMPOOPIN'

Short Stories from 5,000 Words and Longer

THE WEB WE WEAVE

For two weeks now, I've been trying to figure out if people are laughing with me or at me. I'm a sophomore, and I've just run through my financial aid, which wouldn't be a problem, except my asshole father claimed me as a dependent to offset recent alimony payments to my mother. Maybe he's planning on buying his new girlfriend bigger tits with the deduction, because I'm not seeing a cent of it.

"How are you gonna cover next semester?" my roommate Becca asks.

"Maybe I could donate blood," I say through the crunch of Doritos. "Nah, I'm too squeamish for that."

"Maybe you should sleep with the guy in financial aid and persuade him that you have good enough credentials to stay in school," Becca says. She is beautiful with dark features, athletic curves, and guys fall all over themselves to catch a glimpse.

"Maybe I'll cut your hair while you're sleeping and sell it to the cosmetology school for a wig," I reply.

"Go ahead," Becca says, bouncing into our kitchenette. "But be prepared to wake up without eyebrows."

I fold my feet under my lap and grab another handful of chips. "Maybe I can start a nine-hundred-number. Those girls make good money, don't they?"

Becca carries over two diet sodas, handing one to me. "Livy, you can't be a virgin and have phone sex."

Yes, I'm still a virgin. But don't think I'm diseased or completely disgusting looking. It was a choice I made in ninth grade. Believe me, I've had plenty of opportunities to change that choice. I'm pretty cute. I mean, not drop dead gorgeous like Becca, but not many girls are and they still get laid.

"But aren't those women like crippled housewives or single moms?" I ask. "I'm already ahead of the game in that case."

Becca glares at me. "They may be missing an arm or breastfeeding but at least they know how to fuck. You'd be like that camel-riding IT guy in the desert reading a manual to help me figure out why my laptop keeps crashing. It's frustrating for the person on the other end of the line 'cause you don't know how to get the job done."

I roll my eyes, knowing she's right. I would have to watch porn just to know which body parts we are talking about. I shake my head. "I can't believe my fucking dad did this to me."

"Sex is a powerful thing, Livy," Becca says.

"Maybe I can get his new girlfriend to do some phone sex to pay for school. It's the least she could do."

Becca turns on *COPS*. A woman who looks like she hasn't seen a shower in twelve years is attempting to talk with a Houston officer. Her teeth are yellow, the ones left anyway, and her hair reminds me of moldy cotton candy. My mouth drops open. "She's being arrested for prostitution?"

"Hey," Becca says. "Some people are desperate."

"I mean for Chris sakes, someone was not only going to pay to fuck that, but they were willing to go to jail if they got caught."

"You know, Livy," Becca says, turning to face me. "You should sell your virginity."

I look at her. "That's not a bad idea."

She laughs, exposing her pearly whites. "Get the fuck out of here. I'm totally joking."

"No," I say. "That's a great idea. I could auction my virginity like a toaster on EBay. It's brilliant."

"Livy, seriously…"

"Why the hell not? My goods are far more valuable then hers." I point to the walking addiction stooping into the backseat of the cop car. "Of course, once a virgin does it, she's no longer a virgin."

Becca shakes her head. "You're not joking."

"What else can I pull off in two weeks to pay for school short of prostitution? Or lap dancing? At least this way I'm offering a real commodity for the highest bidder. Maybe someone will even make a movie about it. Dakota Fanning can play me in the made for TV movie."

"Livy, prostitution is illegal. You may not look like a crack whore but you're still selling your body."

"Who isn't, Becca? People fuck their way up to the top in every line of work. Why shouldn't I cash in? Guys kill themselves in religions with the promise of virgins waiting in heaven. What I got here is worth a lot of money."

The car drives away and the *COPS* logo appears

on the screen. I have a lot of work to do.

The next day after class I detour to the IT Department to find some kid looking for an extra credit assignment. I figure the best way to get out there is to create a website but I don't speak computer.

But how do you approach someone with this sort of project? Can you candidly just say, *"Hi, I'm Livy and I'm a virgin,"* like I'm at an AA meeting? I jump as a hand taps my shoulder.

"Can I help you?"

I turn and stand face to face with a sandy-blond haired guy wearing horn-rimmed glasses.

"Yeah," I say. "I have a project I need some help with."

"Sure," he says. "Come on over." He walks to his desk like I am just another student looking for a website with flowery language and clever graphics. Well, sort of. There's a flower involved and it is definitely graphic in nature.

We sit at his cluttered desk and I notice a collection of comic books on the bookshelf behind him. Surprise, surprise, a techy with a geeky side. The problem is that he actually isn't a bad looking guy, which makes what I am about to ask so much more difficult.

"I'm Sam," he says. "What can I help you with?"

I lean forward and lower my voice. "Sam, I'm not sure how to say this so I'm just going to be direct."

Sam leans forward mimicking me. "Would it help if I whispered, too?" His eyes are dark blue. I had thought they were brown.

I explain the situation and what I am hoping to

accomplish and sit back, giving Sam a moment to let it sink in. Sam presses his lips together, opens his mouth, but then closes it again without saying anything.

"I knew this was a bad idea," I say.

"I could use a beer. You?" he asks.

"Yes. Definitely."

The pub is just off campus and we take separate cars. C'mon, I didn't want to come across as easy. After a few too many beers we are both talking with our guards down.

"It's not like I don't believe in love," I say through the accent of Corona and lime. "I just don't think it comes in that neat package that I have been saving myself for. I mean, what's the point in waiting for something and giving your life to it, only to have it ripped out from under you for some big-tittied blonde who makes your Viagra worth taking?"

"Do your parents still love each other?"

"How the hell should I know? They were together since high school and then one day, it's over; the friendship, the relationship, the family. Over."

Sam places his hand on mine. "It's not like that for everyone, Livy. My parents got divorced when I was in the tenth grade and I was devastated. I couldn't understand why they just couldn't get their shit together. After a while, I saw my mom smiling again and my dad and I started talking again, really talking. They were both happier." He takes a drink. "What I realized is that although they were my parents, they were two people long before I came into the picture."

Sam moves his hand away. "It wasn't love's fault that their marriage didn't work. It was life. They let it get in the way. But I won't and you don't have to either."

I nod. He is wise for his age, or at least that's what my Corona tells me. But either way, he's right. I slam down my beer and stumble off my stool. "I say yes, yes, to love!" Half the bar turns to stare. Then I yell, "Anyone wanna fuck?"

And that's the last thing I remember.

I open my eyes to lines of light piercing to the back of my skull. Pots and pans rattle somewhere in the house and I smell bacon cooking, which turns my stomach. My head pounds with each pulse and I moan.

Where the hell am I?

I lift my head like a newborn calf. My shoes and socks lay on the floor. Oh shit. It's starting to come back to me. I sit up on the edge of the bed. How the hell did I get so drunk? I look to make sure I'm dressed. Check, thank God. I follow the noise to the kitchen. Sam stands over the stove cooking.

"Hey," he says. "Thought you could use a greasy breakfast." A plate of bacon and eggs sit beside a tall glass of OJ on the kitchen bar. "Coffee?"

"God, yes," I answer.

I nibble some bacon while he pours, enjoying the aroma of hazelnut before it hits my tongue. It's quiet for a moment while he watches me.

Finally, I blurt out, "Did we..."

"No," he answers.

I nod, sipping orange juice.

"So, I worked on some ideas for your website last night," he says, grabbing his laptop. He sits it next to me and clicks some keys. "Look it over and let me know what you think." He swivels the laptop to face me.

In bold print the text scrolls across the top of the screen *Virginity for Sale to the Highest Bidder.* He has listed my statistics and added several flattering photos of me along with entertaining graphics.

"Where did you get these pictures," I ask feeling more like myself as the coffee replaces the beer in my bloodstream.

"From your Facebook page. It's amazing how easy it is to access information on the web, yet people just post it like it's their high school locker."

"It looks good," I say, at a loss for words. I mean, really what do you say in a situation like this?

"I can have it up in five minutes. Then we just wait for hits."

I rub my temples. Am I having a panic attack?

"You sure you're ready for this?" Sam asks.

I think about it for a few minutes. What else can I do? "Fuck it," I say. "Let's do it."

I think I'm going to pass out.

"Okay, it's up," Sam says, staring at me. "You all right?"

I don't say anything at first. "Do you think it's a good idea?"

Sam shrugs. "It is if you want to pay your tuition."

Do I?

He smiles. I hadn't noticed he had dimples earlier. "Come on. I'll take you to your car."

When we reach the pub, I turn to Sam. "Thanks for taking care of me last night," I say. "I don't usually drink like that."

"I hope not," Sam says. "You were pretty trashed."

I kiss his cheek, and step out of his car. "Thanks, Sam. See you around."

But I know I won't.

The following two weeks fly by. My website receives over one-hundred thousand hits and my virginity is up to forty-thousand dollars. I know, who'd have thunk it. I don't see Sam again. But I think about him. A lot, actually.

Why can't I get him out of my head? It was something he said, about how life and not love had gotten in the way of his parents' relationship. I can't shake that thought. And then, just twenty minutes before the close of the auction to sell my virginity, it hits me. That was it. I was letting life get in the way of love. I didn't want to fuck some stranger for money like Yellow-Tooth, the prostitute on *COPS*. I wanted to wait for real love, no matter how fantastic or unattainable that ideal might be.

I drive to Sam's house and pound on his front door.

"Hey, Livy," he says, opening the door. "Is everything okay?"

"I want love!" I blurt out.

Sam stops. "What?"

"I don't want life to get in the way," I say. "I don't want money for school to get in the way of what choices I make with love." I grab Sam's hands. "I don't want to sell to a stranger what I have saved all my life to give to someone I fall in love with. It doesn't matter what choices my parents made. You were right. I don't have to let life get in the way of love. I want you to shut down the website."

Sam stares at me, rubbing his hands through his hair. "Jesus, Livy, you're talking over forty-thousand dollars. You sure you're ready for this?"

I smile. "I've never been so sure of anything in my life."

Sam pulled the website with forty-four thousand, two hundred and eighty-four dollars in bids going unclaimed. It was a hard thing to let go of, but so was my virginity. Luckily, I got a check from my dad two days later for the full tuition cost. Apparently my mom found out about what I was doing and gave my dad an earful. I guess Dad's girlfriend's new tits will have to wait.

So, as I said in the beginning, I've been trying to figure out if people are laughing with me or at me. I mean, I did give up a lot of money. But I don't care. It was worth it. And I'm sure some people are laughing with me because through it all, I did find love, and that's kind of funny considering the circumstances under which Sam and I met.

By the way, I got a letter last week from some producer in California who says he wants to turn my story into one of those Movies of the Week you see on the Hallmark Channel. Can you believe it? I won't ever have to worry about tuition again.

I wonder if Dakota Fanning is available?

The Sword of Kusanagi

(a selection from *Clifton Chase and the Arrow of Light*)

The group of men descended angrily to the base of the mast; fists raised, while shouting and swearing so badly, twelve-year-old Clifton almost covered his own ears. He finally got where the expression 'swears like a sailor' came from. Jeez!

Henry VII rushed to the front of the crowd beneath the crow's nest. His stern face pulled forward in anger, and he lifted his head. "Alfred Mansfield!"

The mob fell silent.

"Alfred Mansfield, show yourself!"

Nothing stirred in the crow's nest.

"Traitor! Coward!" Fourteen-year-old Prince Edward crossed the deck as if wearing his royal robes. "You will return what you have stolen at once and face a sure death by walking the plank."

A hoarse voice drifted down from the crow's nest. "I will do no such thing."

"What is he thinking?" Clifton whispered to Dane, a dwarf with bushy red eyebrows and hair to match. "He's on a ship in the middle of the English Channel, surrounded. He's got no chance."

Dane shook his head. "He's got the Arrow of

Light, lad. You still don't understand? The power is in his hands, if he's not too much of a fool to figure it out."

A cold chill crossed Clifton's skin. Soft voices chimed from the channel, their song familiar in the way a scent can trigger a memory. Unexplainably, he felt a strong pull toward the water and fought the urge to jump in.

A dark image darted below the surface. Then another one. Were they dolphins? They might have been if they were sailing in Florida, but this was the English Channel. Maybe they were porpoises. They'd been known to swim in these cold waters. The images propelled underwater, pacing beneath him. Leaning closer, he pressed his chest against the bough, his feet still touching the deck.

Jasper Tudor crossed the deck to the base of the crow's nest, his head wound tightly inside an ornate cloth. A black robe, decorated with symbols in gold and silver threads, skimmed the deck. In his hand, he held a sword, the hilt shaped into a figure Clifton couldn't make out from the distance. The men whispered, a wave of terror sweeping through the air.

"What is that on the hilt?" Clifton asked.

"It's an eight-headed serpent," nine-year-old Prince Richard said. "That's the sword of Kusanagi."

"The sword of who?"

Richard turned, his baby blue eyes wide. "You do not know the lure?"

Clifton shook his head.

"Quiet!" Dane snapped. "Listen closely."

Richard leaned in under Clifton's nose, a childish grin on his face. "Kusanagi is the Japanese god of storms who slay an eight-headed dragon with that sword, the Sword of the Gathering Clouds of Heaven."

"Pipe down," Dane said, through gritted teeth.

"The sword was used to direct the wind as an assault upon Kusanagi's enemies."

"And Jasper has it?"

Richard nodded, his eyebrows arched and raised, as if preparing to jump off his face. "Jasper is a man of much mystery. You can never be surprised by anything he does."

Jasper chanted in the same language he used to evade a Crestback Dragon when they were back in Èze, a beautiful mountainside town in France. His arms slowly lifted, raising the sword above his head. His palms pressed together with the blade between them, the eight-headed dragon pointed skyward. Kusanagi's sword illuminated, sending blinding light through the air.

"Oh, no," Dane said.

"What?" Clifton asked. "What's happening?"

"I can't be certain," Dane said, taking slow strides backward. "But I think I've heard this one before."

"What does that mean?"

"It means you'd best find something nailed down. And hold on tight." Dane disappeared through the crowd.

Dark clouds rolled in from thin air. Thunder clapped and lightening flashed. The sailors dissipated to man their positions, heaving sails, tightening ropes, and shouting commands. Jasper chanted louder, his voice growing in harmony with the howling winds and threatening storm. Then his eyes glazed over in a milky-white film. He had fallen into a trance; the conjurer of the storm.

Clifton dodged the wind, searching for something to brace against. The rocking ship knocked him off-balance as he strained to keep his footing. Large waves crashed against the hull and spilled over the sides drenching the deck. In desperation, Clifton grabbed hold of a heavy rope anchored to the sidewall and held on for his life. Pandemonium swelled, the rushing sailors hollering, fighting with the slick deck to stay grounded. Rain poured down in heavy streams and the ship quaked, rocking in sharp angles; the crow's nest bent like a palm tree in a hurricane.

Jasper was trying to shake Alfred out.

The idea was brilliant, really. Tethered against the rope, Clifton braced hard, squinting against the stinging rain, shoving toward the base of the mast. He had almost made it when the boat dropped so deep Clifton panicked, thinking it would capsize.

Through the darkness, a light glowed, not from the Sword of the Gathering Clouds of Heaven, but from something else. The diamond tip of the Arrow of Light poked through the center of the coiled pile of thick rope Clifton held to stay onboard. It swayed, a snake dancing for a charmer, the shaft brilliant against the black clouds and rain.

Clifton pulled harder and lunged toward the arrow when he was close enough. A massive wave struck the hull. Lightning cracked the mast, snapping off the crow's nest, sending it toppling to the deck with a hard crash. Grabbing the arrow with one hand, Clifton's other hand cramped around the slick, knotted fibers of the rope.

The ship shifted and his grip slipped off the rope,

knocking him to the deck, his head smacking against the wood. He saw stars. The ship corrected, rolling too far in the opposite direction, shuffling Clifton like an air hockey puck to the opposite edge. He rolled over the wooden handrail and plunged on his back toward the sea. Lighting flashed. And before he hit the water, he watched Alfred Mansfield tumbling over the handrail, heading straight for him.

Clifton slammed the channel's surface, the water so cold it snatched his breath away. His muscles became rigid as he plunged deeper, the arrow clenched in his fist. He twisted to face what he hoped was up. But the sea and clouds soaked up the light like a black hole. He forced his legs to kick, his arms to tread, as he swam for the top before his burning lungs gave way. In a final burst, he broke through the channel's skin, gulping hungry breaths. He blinked through the rain, his eyes darting. Where was Alfred?

Two large hands pressed on his shoulders from behind, shoving Clifton underwater before he could take in a full breath. He squirmed away and kicked off to the side. Clifton shot back up to the surface. Alfred waded a few feet away.

"Give me that back," Alfred yelled, lurching at the arrow and grabbing Clifton by the wrist. He was much stronger than Clifton, whose wrist ached from twisting and bending.

With his free hand, Clifton swung at Alfred's head, punching him over and over again. Alfred released his grip with a yelp. Clifton kicked off the man's gut and swam far away.

Clifton looked up to the ship. Many of the sailors leaned over the railing watching. Dane shouted, pointing into the distance. Although the storm was dying down, Clifton could not understand him. What was he pointing at?

Clifton scanned the sea. Two scaly islands rolled in and out of the channel, seemingly disconnected. They went under. Something slimy brushed his leg. Clifton kicked, hoping it was one of the creatures he had seen swimming earlier and not a sea serpent. What if it was? What in the world was he supposed to do? He could never out swim one, let alone get away from Alfred first. Clifton focused on the figures singing so beautifully to him, convincing himself they were the scaly humps he had seen.

Not likely.

Alfred didn't seem to notice or care what those humps were either way. He was too busy screaming over the storm. "You'll pay for that." He dove into the waves.

Clifton swam hard for the ship when Alfred yanked his leg and pulled him under. Clifton sucked in as much air as he could. Underwater, he opened his eyes. The salt burned briefly and the murky water clouded everything outside of an arm's length.

Alfred clamped Clifton's leg, pulling him closer, wrestling for possession of the arrow. Something massive swam past them with a shriek. The look on Alfred's face spread terror through Clifton's blood. He used the fraction of a second to fight the man off, but Alfred quickly recovered, his hand like a vice grip pinching Clifton's flesh.

Clifton didn't know how much longer he could hold on. The water was too cold and his muscles were failing. Then he remembered something Dane had said about the arrow, when they had first left his cottage to rescue the princes. He could almost hear his voice:

"Attaches itself to its chosen possessor...passes on protection and wisdom."

Of course. He held the Arrow of Light, forged by Time herself from the Tree of Knowledge; an insurance policy guaranteeing long life, protection, and wisdom. If he only knew how it worked. He clenched his fist tighter around the shaft, wondering how to unlock its power. Alfred wrapped his hands around Clifton's neck, pressing on his windpipe. Clifton concentrated on the arrow, begging it to help him. His throat burned, his mind muddled as Alfred pressed harder.

"Please, help me," Clifton thought, pleading with the arrow to come to life. Clifton's eyes rolled back. The shaft did not glow. Even in the current, the copper-colored feathers that belonged to Simurgh, the great bird of Wisdom, looked still as wood.

He was going to die here.

The water around them began to shudder as great waves rippled and swirled. There was a rush of water. The sea serpent. If he could just twist around, he might be able to use Alfred as a buffer. Maybe even bait. With much effort, Clifton kicked his legs to maneuver them around. Humps in the water grew closer, just off Alfred's right shoulder, and with a jerk, Alfred's hands were ripped away as his body was dragged off. All that was left of the man was his scream in a trail of lingering bubbles.

The shock waves continued and Clifton tumbled, as he had many times in the surf on Melbourne Beach back home in Florida. The long tail of the sea serpent appeared in front of him swishing like a humongous eel in the water. It turned around immediately, as if folding in half. It was coming back for Clifton. Its many heads faced him staring with mouths gaping, mouths that had just devoured Alfred. He didn't count the number of heads as he tumbled, but he would have bet there were eight.

With all the faith he could find, he begged the arrow to help him. He challenged its power, trying to believe its purpose for choosing Clifton was for something far greater than this creature's dinner.

Within reach of the monster's jagged teeth, Clifton screamed, releasing his last air reserves. If he was going to die here, he'd rather drown than be eaten. The serpent's eight jaws hinged open; the suctioning water pulled Clifton in. The mouths were like vast caverns of black oil. This was it. The end. Then, something grabbed him from behind. Whatever it was, it pulled him out of the vortex at an unbelievable speed.

The monster closed its jaws and faded into blackness. Clifton sped backward, desperate for air. Moving farther away from the monster, the ship, his friends, and consciousness, deep down into the black sea.

Clifton was seconds away from passing out when a slender hand secured a gelatinous device to his face. It shrank to fit, suctioning to his forehead, cheeks, and chin. He could see through it, the material resembling a jellyfish, and without choice he sucked in a deep breath.

And he could breathe.

The jellyfish-mask was some sort of organic breathing device. *Thank God*. With that problem solved, he now wondered who or what was pulling him and where they were taking him.

It wasn't a sea serpent. The slender hand which covered his face could never be attached to something so hideous. He remembered the figures he had seen earlier, swimming below the ship's deck before all the chaos with the storm and Alfred. It had to be one of those creatures which rescued him from those eight hungry mouths; he somehow felt comforted. Maybe they were friendly after all.

Resonating through the black waters, a melody sang clearly as a tinkling of crystal glasses. Clifton thought of his mother tucking him into bed at night when he was little. And of his baby brother, Pierce, when he caught a fit of giggles. And of his father during their trips alone fishing, when they talked for hours until the sun set.

Slowly, light filtered through from somewhere beneath him. Clifton tried to turn his body to look below but couldn't. His captor's grip held too strong.

"Be still, Clifton Chase," a strange voice sang in his head.

As they swam, the light intensified and Clifton glimpsed a seaweed forest. Tall mountains surrounded them as they passed through a canyon covered in beautifully colored corals and swaying sea plants in bloom. The landscape was enchanting, and without the water, Clifton thought the view would be the same here as his pass through the forests and mountains of Èze.

The tops of large structures appeared, jutting up like stalagmites through the dense seaweed forest. Clifton was taken lower, through the seaweed beds, and he couldn't see for a moment, as when descending in an airplane through clouds.

When the forest cleared, Clifton gasped. He darted over an ancient city. Massive coral pillars lined the open streets where schools of fish swam freely, and seahorses pulled chariots. Square buildings, resembling ancient Roman architecture, bordered the open design of the cityscape.

Closer still, he could make out the details of a paved shell road intersecting the city's center leading to the steps of a palace. Clifton couldn't believe what he saw. And even more impressive than the underwater city were its inhabitants. Swimming in the water and riding on the seahorse-drawn chariots, and most assuredly the species of the creature pulling Clifton from behind, were unmistakably mermaids.

They lowered Clifton to the seafloor and released. He realized he could be in for another adventure, but at least for now he was safe from that sea serpent. A crowd of merpeople gathered, no longer singing, and Clifton tightened his grasp on the Arrow of Light. Standing on either side of him were his kidnappers. Or maybe they were his savioris.

He'd have to wait and see.

The Outlander

(a selection from *Dreadlands: Wolf Moon*)

They weren't far from the river when Toov's howl flooded the air.

"What was that?" Bane asked, tensed.

"That was my grandmother," Arud said, his moss toned eyes scanning the woods. "She's shifted again, and has taken my sister, Lykke."

"How can you be sure it was her?"

"I know her howl. She's been stalking us since we first left the Outlands."

"What do we do?" Bane asked, his bald head reflecting the faint winter sun.

Several howls answered Toov's in the distance. Dense trees patched in tight clumps hindered Arud's view through the forest. "We get ready. She is gathering her pack."

"How many do you think?" Ek asked, rubbing his peppered beard.

"I don't know, Father. But, if Lykke is as important as the prophecy says, then we could be facing an army of ferine."

"That's not good, boy," Bane said.

Arud didn't respond.

"Well, let's stop standing around like prey and gear up," Ek said. He loaded his crossbow then wedged a knife into his belt. His long spear leaned against a birch tree off to the side.

At least thirty bolts welded of pure silver filled Bane's quiver. Arud unlatched his crossbow and notched a silver bolt of his own. His hands trembled as another round of howls sounded in the distance.

"I hear at least three," Bane said.

"Then prepare for ten," Ek told him. "Circle up. Back to back."

They huddled together, collectively able to watch every angle of the surrounding woods. The howling echoed eerily through the trees; ferine calling and answering in a shrill song. Sweat formed across Arud's brow. How could they ever survive this? The stillness of the forest seemed to grow louder.

"They are coming," Ek said.

"No," Arud said. "They're already here."

A pair of familiar red eyes glowed in the dark shadows between the trees facing Arud.

"I see three," Bane said.

"I see two more," Ek added.

"And I see my grandmother," Arud seethed.

"Take aim, but wait until they are within range," Bane said.

"Tell me, Arud," Ek said over his shoulder, "how do we defeat our enemy?"

"By letting them think they've won, then striking when they least expect it."

"Good. Remember, your blood also holds value to the ferine. Bane and I will take out as many as we can, but it's unlikely we will survive."

"That's encouraging," Arud said.

"You *should* feel encouraged. Toov will not let her pack harm you. Lure her in. Make her think you have given up. Then kill her."

Arud swallowed gravel, his pulse pounding in his ears.

Two identical snow white ferine appeared first through the glade, followed by a smaller one with a yellow coat. Toov stepped out of the shadows, her massive bulk sending chills across Arud's flesh. Red eyes burned as hot embers. Sharp teeth called out for blood. Her black fur glistened, the silver strands running through like veins, pulsating as if alive. The rest of the pack prowled behind her, their pointed ears alert, their long legs pacing.

"What are they doing?" Bane asked.

"I don't know," Arud said. "Maybe they sense our silver."

"Then now is the time to strike," Ek said, pulling his bowstring to full draw.

He released three bolts in one snap, two landing in the red ferine's side, the other missing its mark. The ferine yelped, its body smoking from the silver. In a vicious fury, the pack attacked, fangs bared, foam dripping from their pointed muzzles. Arud struck the white one and Bane's bolt caught its twin. The howling ferine did not die immediately, but the silver disabled them, giving Arud, Ek, and Bane time to gather stray bolts and reload.

The red ferine recovered quickly and launched through the air pushing Bane to the ground. He sliced his blade at the creature, splattering its black blood across the snow, the effects of the silver bubbling the beast's muscles and tissues. The ferine bit Bane's hand and he cut inside its mouth till its ragged jaw hung only by stretched skin at the hinge. It jerked back. Bane slipped underneath and sliced its belly. Intestines piled out into a steaming heap on the snowy forest floor. The ferine collapsed, then shifted back into its human form; the outline of a long-haired woman all that remained.

Ek tramped upon the yellow ferine pinned to the ground by his bolts. The ferine slashed its sharp retractable claws at Ek, who used his spear to stab into its narrow chest over and over again cracking bones, piercing muscle, puncturing organs. A last wheeze rattled from the beast's throat before it ceased moving and began its shift. As Ek withdrew his weapons from the carcass, the white twin pounced on his back barreling him to the ground. Its teeth tore into Ek's flesh and he screamed in agony, unable to roll away.

"Father!"

Arud notched his crossbow, launching bolt after bolt upon the white ferine, its body writhing and smoking, gradually shifting back to human form. It was not dead yet, the halfling sprawled naked on the ground barely able to breathe.

Arud stood over her. "Where is Lykke? Where is my sister?"

The wide-eyed shifter stared up at him, and hissed through grinding teeth, "She is one of us now."

"No!" Arud shouted, unsheathing his long knife.

He hacked off her head, watching as it spun down the steep slope. He glanced over at Ek. He was not moving. In a blur, the second white ferine charged.

Arud ducked, and the creature flew overhead slamming into a tree. The dazed ferine wandered away before returning, shaking its head.

"Bane! White!"

Bane stopped hacking at the corpse of the yellow ferine and turned his eyes on the white one. Together, Arud and Bane took aim on either side of the white demon, shooting three bolts each into its muscular body. The disoriented ferine attempted to charge, staggering back and forth from Bane to Arud, until finally, overcome by the silver, she collapsed at Bane's feet.

"Get the others," Bane shouted, slicing off the ferine's head just as it began its metamorphosis.

Arud turned. Corpses of human women, the transformed versions of all the ferine in the Outlands, lay scattered across the ground. But, two teenage boys about Arud's age lay alongside them.

Just like the Prophecy spoke would happen in the end times.

Toov stood sentinel beside the sandy ferine who growled threateningly exposing bloody gums and fangs, pawing frantically at the snow. Toov appeared to be hampering her attack. Arud glanced at his father. He still hadn't moved.

"Bane, check Ek."

Bane lurched over, covered in black blood mixed with his own, and felt for a pulse. "He's alive!"

Arud closed his eyes, nodding compulsively. "Stay with him, Bane. The black ferine is mine." Arud advanced upon Toov. "Where is Lykke? What have you done with her?"

A sick smile crept across Toov's canine lips.

Arud notched a bolt, aiming it at his grandmother. "Where is she?"

Toov nudged the sandy ferine she guarded.

Arud shook his head. "No. No! That's not my sister." But, then, Arud peered into the ferine's bloodshot, hazel eyes and glimpsed Lykke; beneath the fur, beneath the evil possessing her. His shoulders slumped forward. "What've you done to her?"

Lykke snapped sharp teeth in the air drooling in her bloodlust, her eyes locked on Arud's.

Arud faced Toov. "You can't have her. I'm not afraid of you anymore."

As if to prove her dominance, Toov swatted at Lykke, sending the small ferine hurdling through the air. She slammed into a tree with a painful squeal before her body fell lifeless to the snow.

Arud screamed, releasing his bolt. Toov turned, growling from deep within as she attacked Arud; battering him, leveling him to the ground. Together, they tumbled across the forest floor, her teeth tearing at his flesh, his knife shredding through her thick pelt. Her weighty body crushed him with every roll. How was he going to get the upper hand?

Let her think she's won.

Their momentum slowed and Toov wasted no time pinning Arud down, her nails like a grapnel digging deep into his shoulders, drawing blood. He howled in agony. She barked, spraying bloodstained saliva and spittle across his face. Bane's footfalls grew nearer. "Stay back!" Arud shouted, but Bane wouldn't listen.

Bane released two bolts, both landing in Toov's side where they smoldered, her silvery fur rippling.

She screeched a piercing howl and turned rabid eyes upon Bane while leaping off of Arud and charging at her new target. Bane notched a fresh bolt, but not before Toov plunged into his chest, her claws swatting and slicing in erratic sweeps. Bane fell to the ground, his chest baring freshly carved red stripes.

"Hey!" Arud shouted. "Leave him alone. It's me you want!"

Toov jerked her bloody muzzle in Arud's direction. He drew back the string on his notched crossbow. "I know you need my blood to fulfill the prophecy. But, you can't have it. You and your kind will not live to see another full moon." Arud's bolt bulleted through the air and Toov leapt out of the way, catching the silver tip in her muscular back leg. As she pivoted, he reloaded and took aim, ready for the final assault that would take her life, when a blur off to the side caught his attention.

A jet black ferine edged from the shadows of the trees, and Arud's heart fell. He knew he wasn't solely capable of fending off two ferine. But he wouldn't be easily defeated. He braced for the new foe but she didn't attack. Instead, she slunk directly to Lykke and nudged her awake. Arud sensed a familiarity surrounding this ferine. He recognized her, in the same manner he recognized Lykke in her shifted form. And with a rush of warmth he understood who protected his little sister.

It was Scalvia, the beautiful girl who had stolen his heart, Scalvia, who was called by the Prophecy to protect him and his sister, Scalvia, the Cur, spawned from ferine and human, who stood fierce and boding before him as a ferine.

Toov growled as her eyes fixated on Scalvia who rumbled back, placing herself as a shield before Lykke. Toov charged and Arud felt time slow to a crawl. Toov's muscles tensed. She sprung in long strides at Scalvia who snarled and barked, still somehow the beautiful girl with long black hair in Arud's eyes. Lykke lay helpless, shifted back to her sweet self, her fur in clumps beside her, her pale curls veiling her face. Something inside of him raged, filling him with a strength that melted his despair.

He released his draw.

The bolt caught in Toov's side.

Then another.

The impact threw her off-balance.

Scalvia leapt. Arud raced closer, hammering another bolt into his grandmother.

Toov and Scalvia collided midair, hurtling to the ground. Toov sunk serrated teeth into Scalvia's flesh, and raked needlelike claws across her skin. Scalvia clashed back with all her might, but she was outrivaled.

Toov was going to kill her.

Arud scanned the battlefield and noticed Ek's long spear. That was it, his only hope to save Scalvia. He grasped it, sprinting close enough to launch the silver shaft. Scalvia's whines were almost too much to bear. In the midst of it all, Lykke stood, staring at Scalvia as Toov ripped her to shreds. Lykke slowly slipped closer as Toov continued her barrage of claw and teeth. Lykke glided nearer. Arud raced faster. What would she do? Would Lykke help Scalvia? Or was she under Toov's command? Had his grandmother succeeded in convincing his sister to fight with the ferine? Arud rushed harder as Lykke shimmied closer. Toov clamped her teeth around Scalvia's neck.

He wasn't going to make it.

Arud couldn't bear to lose them both; the two girls he loved. But, he was too late. Scalvia went limp. Lykke reached for Scalvia, but then, Toov extended her arm, grazing Lykke's chest and neck with her lethal claws.

Arud hoisted back the spear as Lykke spun around onto her stomach, wounded. Arud roared, slicing the spearhead through Toov's spine and chest. His brute force surpassed human capabilities. Animal instinct had overtaken him; growing muscles pressed against his taut skin ready to burst. As he ran, he felt his skin stretch and peel. His bones shifted and his muscles tensed pushing him faster. His eyes pressed closer together as his vision opened; the darkness barely noticeable. He ran on all fours; his breathing deepened, his pulse exploded.

Toov writhed on her hind legs flailing at the spear with her front claws, abandoning Scalvia who began to shift. Toov collapsed on the snow as her blood pooled beneath her. Arud bounded with a monstrous leap through the air, and Toov turned in time to see him flying at her. For the first time, her eyes were filled with terror.

Arud pinned her, his own body towering over hers. The hand he held against her chest was covered in silver fur. Thick silver blades had replaced his nails. His muscles had tripled in size.

He was a ferine.

Arud angled over her. Every coldblooded way he would hurt Toov, for murdering his mother, for afflicting Scalvia, for capturing Lykke, all of it rushed from his heart, as he pushed his claws out several inches longer.

"This is for murdering my mother," he growled, and he sliced her from ear to ear. Toov's head thwacked the ground, and what was left of the black and silver ferine shifted back into the form of Arud's grandmother, Toov.

Bane hobbled over to Scalvia clutching his chest. He carefully removed his cloak, drew in air through clenched teeth, and covered Scalvia's bare body laying several yards from Arud. "She's dying," Bane said, searching for a pulse "They're all dying."

Toov managed to fulfill the prophecy: Lykke's blood had been spilled.

Arud's body swiftly changed back to his human form, bones breaking and mending, fur clumping and pushed off by his growing skin. He cracked his figure to an upright position so he could run over to Lykke, as his cuts and tears instantly healed upon his flesh. Tears fell onto his sister's bloody face. "Lykke, can you hear me?" She did not respond. Her neck bent acutely to the side.

Bane gawked at Toov with a smirk. "I think it's safe to say this one's dead."

"We're taking her head with us to the Capital City," Arud said, "as a warning to her followers."

Lykke moaned. Arud cradled her against his chest. "Please, God. Don't let her die."

But, it wasn't just her. It was his mother and his father. And Scalvia. He couldn't lose them all. What point would there be in living? No family. No amazing girl whose gray eyes he'd get lost in.

Scalvia's chest rose in steady breaths, but she still hadn't stirred. "Don't let her die, either." He continued rocking Lykke in his arms, running his fingers through her curls. "Please don't leave me," he whispered.

She coughed and her eyes fluttered open. She tried speaking, but couldn't.

"Shhhh," Arud whispered, kissing her forehead. "Don't talk. Everything is going to be okay."

Lykke shut her eyes again and Arud sighed. She was going to be all right. Scalvia gasped and Bane stared at her mending arm. "Her wounds are healing. How can that be?"

"She is Cur, Bane. Like Lykke. Of ferine and human blood."

They sat in the woods, bloodied from battle, as both girls rapidly healed. Ek lay stone still and Arud's chest ached, hoping Ek could hold out a little longer. Arud closed his eyes. Tears seeped out the edges as he looked heavenward.

The final battle drew near, and when it came, they would be ready. With Toov destroyed, her army of ravenous ferine would be hungry for revenge. But, they no longer possessed Lykke, the Cur child, the child of the prophecy. Arud had saved his sister from pledging allegiance with the darkness and soon everyone in the Outlands would be safe to travel, even amidst a full moon. Scalvia stirred. Lykke opened her eyes. Arud smiled.

They were going to be all right.

CEREAL KILLER: THE LEPRECHAUN MURDER

The body of world-famous Lucky the Leprechaun was discovered today floating facedown in a large pool of Ne and 2% milk.

"It's a tragedy," said long-time friend Saccharine Slap Bear. "And on Saint Patty's Day!"

Lucky is survived by green clovers, blue diamonds, and purple horseshoes.

My name is Robbie Brown and I am a product icon detective in the homicide division. This story is not for the lactose intolerant, but it's one that must be told.

As I scoped the scene, I noticed Lucky's little green coat was askew, as if he put it on in a hurry. "Get him out of that milk. He's getting soggy."

The Cobbler Elves worked the crane controls while Papa Elf guided the scooper to Lucky's lifeless body. He was lifted, lowered, and left on the grass behind his beautiful bay home. I knelt beside him, right away finding the first thing out of place. "Where's his Lucky Tokens?"

"No clue." That was my partner, Lucas Eagle, who knelt down beside me. "What do you think happened to them, Robbie?"

I didn't answer. Something wasn't clicking. That jacket looked soft. Too soft. Like it had been cleaned right before the leprechaun was dumped.

"Who would wear their jacket to take a swim?" Lucas asked.

"He wasn't taking a swim. We're dealing with a Cereal Killer."

"How can you tell?"

"They left a clue." I pointed to the amber-colored goo beneath Lucky's left lapel.

Lucas touched it. "What is it?"

"Syrup. This was a mob hit, and I bet it will lead us back to Aunt Jemafia."

Aunt Jemafia is the leader of the mob. Known for her brutal use of syrup torture in the 90s, she spread out and employed other products to do her sticky bidding. In 2002, she hired the Nezfast Bunny to lace the chocolate Fast at the governor's ball, though we could never link her to the crime. A brief partnership with Little Suzie led to the cupcake queen's disappearance for several months, after the reveal of her saucy affair with Chef Deearboy. The mob leader was never at a loss for icon henchmen, what with the economy being at an all time-low and breakfast cereal over four-dollars a box, most icons were looking for some extra cash to pay the bills.

Later that day, I sat eating a bowl of Honey-Os while watching the TV. I never buy the brand name stuff. Can't stand those flat-box, beady eyes staring at me while I eat. Not to mention the surveillance technology built into every box ever since Lenny the Lion was busted for slipping steroids into Flaky Frosts.

As I slurped my milk, I couldn't help but wonder what happened to those Lucky Tokens. I'd have to hit the streets for answers.

The Creamy Queen Bar was the hot spot for product icons. Everyone from the Softbooty Bears to the Scare-Berry Monster hung out there. First on my list of suspects was the Daddy Crunch. His gig had gone south, replaced by Cookie the Dog, who was fired for peeing on the cereal, and then Cookie the Wolf, because the FDA deemed the thief image too negative for a kid's cereal. He sat at the bar, a good forty-pounds heavier, with a shot of milk, a plate of fig newtons, and a half gallon of whole milk left behind by the bartender.

"Evening, Mr. Crunch," I said.

"Scram, Copper. I ain't taking the rap."

"I haven't accused you of anything." I sat beside him. "Sure sound mighty guilty."

"You're looking to blame someone for the Cereal Killer's work."

"What do you know?"

"I don't know nothing." He downed his shot and poured another. "And even if I did, I wouldn't tell you anything."

I stared him down, waiting for him to crumble.

He faced me. "I don't know why you're bothering me. I've been clean for three years. Ain't stole a single chocolate-chip cookie from no one. Stopped eating them completely. Made a new life for myself."

"And you should be proud of that. But I'm sure you still hear things, having a reputation of working for Aunt Jemafia on more than one occasion."

"Scram." He shoos me aside. "Beat it. Unless

you've got a warrant."

I hadn't one, so I stood and whispered in his good ear. "A leprechaun's dead, and that means anyone could be next. Even retired icons like yourself. Cereal Killers don't care if you've deserted your box or not."

As I turned to leave, he grabbed my wrist, stopping me in my moose tracks. "You didn't hear this from me," he whispered, "but that silly rabbit has worked the streets for the mob for years. They pay him in Tricks. It's the only way he can eat his own cereal."

"Pretty twisted. Heard he's only actually eaten it twice: once back in '76 and once in the 80s."

"It is twisted, and enough to drive an icon to do things they wouldn't normally do, if you buy what I'm selling." He released me. "But you didn't hear it from me."

I reached into my pocket and laid two chocolate-chip cookies on the bar. "Thanks for your time." On the way out, I video called Lucas. "Any idea where to find the Tricks Bunny?"

"He's been picked up a few times for shoplifting and harassing the kids down near the river. Lost his home back in the 90s after the market crashed."

"Grab a few boxes of Tricks and meet me near Riverfront Playground. I've got a call to make."

Little Suzie lived in a small treetop trailer park on the outskirts of town. She'd shagged up with an ex-Cobbler elf turned diabetic who ate too much product and could no longer perform his duties. The two lived off his disability checks and the dwindling cash reserves she had leftover from selling her cupcake conglomerate. Cobwebs cluttered the corners of the door frame. I knocked gingerly.

"Hold you horses," came a hoarse voice from behind the wood door. It opened on rusty hinges. Little Suzie wore a flannel nightshirt to her knees and fuzzy slippers, her short hair wound tight in curlers. "Can I help you?" A cigarette teetered between her lips as she spoke, and she removed it only to cough.

"I'm Officer Brown." I flashed my badge. "I'm looking for information on the Cereal Killer. You heard of him?"

She shrugged. "I watch the news."

"Do you know the whereabouts of the Tricks Bunny?"

"I'm sorry, Officer, but am I being accused of something? Cause I'm a very busy woman."

"The theory is this was a mob hit. You know of Aunt Jemafia, don't you?"

She blew out a dark chocolate-hued cloud of smoke. "Come inside."

We sat in the center room attached on one side to a small kitchenette. A slim hallway led to a bedroom and bath at the other end. A bald-headed elf sat in a wheelchair facing the TV. One of his legs had been amputated at the knee.

"Bernie," Little Suzie said louder than necessary. "We have company."

The elf swiveled around. I showed my badge. He ignored me after that.

"Cup of Joe?" Little Suzie asked, holding out the pot. I nodded, and she poured for each of us. We silently stirred in our cream and sugar. The scent of coffee lingered among the cigarettes Little Suzie chain smoked, but the scent of flowers layered subtly beneath it all. I wondered why.

"Not so long ago, Aunt Jemafia and I were the best of friends," Little Suzie began. "We were like sisters. But her syrup got to her head and she ruined my reputation. I was forced to sell my business, my house, everything I owned. Gone." She dragged off her newly lit cigarette. "After that, no one would work with me. No one would even talk to me, except Bernie, which isn't saying much."

"What about Chef Deearboy?"

She snorted. "That creep? He swore by his meatballs that he loved me and would leave that frozen-hearted Mary Kalandeer. But after I lost my swiss cake rolls, he left me. Said he couldn't be with someone without dough in their future."

"Wanted his cake and to eat it too, huh?"

"That's right. Anyway, none of this would have happened if that Mrs. Buttervalue wannabe hadn't opened her big fat lid and blabbed to the whole world about me and the Chef."

"Do you think she's got something to do with the Cereal Killer?"

"Could be. She's got a gambling problem; owes dough all over town, mostly to Betty Crockpot and Orville Rumplesbottom."

"Interesting." I jotted names in my notebook. "Any idea if the Rabbit plays in?"

"He's a junkie. Will do anything for Tricks."

"Even commit murder?"

"Especially. All you need to know is his weakness."

I'd heard all I needed. I stood and said, "Thanks for your information."

"Anything to get Aunt Jemafia busted."

"I'll let myself out." As I walked to the door, I wondered if Little Suzie was involved. She had motive, but until I could prove it I had nothing. I headed toward the playground, hoping Lucas had brought a lot of breakfast cereal.

Riverfront Playground stayed open from dawn to dusk. Typical equipment and wooden benches created a commonplace ambiance no different from any park anywhere in the country. Lucas sat on the swings, a black duffle bag on the sand beside him.

"Thanks for meeting me."

"What's this all about, Robbie?"

"I'm not certain yet."

"You think the rabbit did it?"

"I think the rabbit was put up to it." I cupped my hands to my mouth. "Silly Rabbit? ILPD. We just want to talk."

Nothing stirred. I faced Lucas. "You got the Tricks?"

Lucas unzipped the duffle bag. Lemon-lime and orange zest and raspberry filled the air. "I give him one minute."

The door to the playground tree-house swung opened. A white creature with long ears dragged across the wood chips.

"Is that him?" Lucas asked.

"It must be. But he's got to be at least thirty pounds lighter."

The Rabbit approached, the streetlamps cast creepy shadows across his sunken cheeks and bloodshot eyes. "You got Tricks?" he muttered.

Lucas quickly zipped the bag closed. "That depends on your answers."

The Rabbit tried to run, but Lucas and I were on top of him like the graham crackers on a s'mores. "Let go of me!" the Rabbit screamed.

"Why'd you kill Lucky?" I asked.

"I didn't kill no one."

"You're lying!" Lucas said.

"No…no, please…let me go!"

"You talk, or we'll feed you to the Goldfishes."

"PLEASE! Anything but that. I don't know nothing!"

Lucas and I carried the Rabbit to the dock and hung him upside down over the river. His ears dragged on the surface. Instantly, the Pepperidge Farm Piranha jumped in the air and clamped their teeth around the Rabbit's stringy ears. He yowled in pain.

"Who killed Lucky? Was it you? Did Aunt Jemafia put you up to it?"

"No. It wasn't me. He was dead when I got there. Just get me away from the Piranha."

Lucas and I brought the Rabbit back to the park and sat him on a bench to catch his breath. "Who sent you?"

"Aunt Jemafia told me to meet her there."

"Why?"

The Rabbit shrugged. "Didn't say."

Lucas pushed the duffle bag closer. The Rabbit's eyes glazed over. I shoved a handful of Tricks into my mouth, and so did Lucas.

"She said she needed me to steal Lucky's pot of gold to pay off her gambling debts, all right?"

"To who? Betty and Orville?"

"I don't know."

Lucas and I ate more cereal. I chewed with my

mouth opened.

"The Puffstuff Roll Boy." Lucky finally caved.

"That puff? He's got plenty of dough," Lucas said.

"Yeah, but he loaned a crescent rollful to Aunt Jemafia so she could buy out the Little Suzie snack company under a false name."

I shook my head. "This doesn't make any sense. Why would Aunt Jemafia incriminate herself? Why would she tell so much to a junkie like you, and then bail out?"

"No idea, man. Go talk to her. Maybe she's schizo and has a double personality or something. Could you just give me the Tricks already?"

Lucas zipped the duffle bag and swung it over his shoulder. The Rabbit stared at us as we walked away. "So that's it? What about my Tricks? You promised me you'd give me some if I talked."

I smirked. "Silly, Rabbit. Tricks are for kids."

We left the poor fool pounding his head in the sand, screaming, yanking at his own ears. I felt bad, but I knew in the long run we were doing him a favor. At least that's what I told myself.

I sent Lucas back to the station to check on forensics. Hopefully, the lab was able to turn something up. I headed to Aunt Jemafia's pancake flat in the downtown district. I rang the bell and she greeted me, as if she knew I was coming. The scent of waffles fell out of the house.

"Detective Brown, what brings you here? Breakfast for dinner?"

She'd put on a few pats of butter since I last saw her. "I'm looking for information about the Cereal Killer and your possible connection."

She laughed. "I figured you'd show up at my door eventually. Who was it? That strung out Rabbit? Or that Tarah Dee tart Little Suzie?"

"Both. They say you owe money all over town, and that most of it belongs to the dough boy who lent it so you could take out your competition."

"Little Suzie has never been my competition."

"Then why'd you buy her out under a fake name?"

"You can't believe everything you hear."

"I don't care either way. I'm just looking for justice."

"Well, I was here all day yesterday and I can get Da'boss Frog and Steinberry to validate."

"I don't believe it was you."

"Then why are you here?"

"Because I think someone is framing you, and I haven't decided if you're in on it or not."

Her face etched with lines of rage. "Well unless you have a warrant you need to get off my property." She slammed the door in my face. But as she did, the same scent of flowers I smelled at Little Suzie's seeped out.

Why in the world would they both have the same smell? My phone rang. It was Lucas. "Tell me something good."

"The residue on the Leprechaun's jacket was definitely syrup, but not Aunt Jemafia's. And that's not all."

"What else?"

"Traces of ethyl acetate, ethanol, and benzyl alcohol were found around the syrup. What does it mean?"

Chemicals? Foreign syrup? I thought hard,

reminded of the flowery scent at both houses. Suddenly, I gasped. "I know who did it."

Lucas and I met back at Little Suzie's house. She opened the door. Smoke haloed her head like a honey-nut Cheerio.

"What now? You come here to tell me you arrested that Silly Rabbit?"

"Actually, we came to search the place." I flashed my warrant.

Little Suzie's face went red velvet and she screeched. "What in the world? You think I had the Leprechaun drowned? You think I stole his Lucky Tokens."

I smiled widely. *Bingo.* "I never mentioned they were missing."

The cupcake queen went quiet as Lucas and I pushed past her to search the trailer. I went straight to her laundry room and opened the dryer. Lucky's charms spilled out onto the floor. Lucas handcuffed Little Suzie and read her her rights while the elf stared at the television screen as if nothing was happening.

As we lowered her into the squad car, Little Suzie said, "How'd you know it was me?"

"The fabric softener. I smelled it at your place and at Aunt Jemafia's. I figured maybe it was the Cuddle Bear who'd been hired by the mob, but turns out he has a summer home in Venice where he's at right now. That left the puzzle of why both houses smelled like flowers, but then I got it. You laundered money for the mob. Washed and dried Lucky's pot of gold for Aunt Jemafia, but you got caught in the act. The Leprechaun showed up while you were doing the deed so you off-ed him. The question is why."

Little Suzie stared up, tears streaming down her pink cheeks. "She said she'd give me my company back. I can't keep living like this, in a piece of crap trailer park with a useless diabetic elf who can't get a job and has a terrible drinking problem. I just wanted my life back."

"So you took Lucky's life? Don't you know you can't have your cake and eat it too?"

"I just wanted a fresh start."

"You'll get a fresh start, sharing a jail cell with Aunt Jemafia. Maybe the two of you can clean up your acts. Mr. Cleaner heads up the parole board, so you'd better make sure you wash behind your ears when your time comes."

As the patrolman drove Little Suzie away, I grabbed a laundry bag and filled it with Lucky's charms. The streets were safe again for product icons with the Cereal Killers headed to prison. Just another day's work for a guy like me...Officer Robbie Brown, ILPD.

THE BOMBASTIC ADVENTURES OF BOB FROM PLANET 9

Melvin and Bob sat at their usual table, the floater in the glass bubble with the view of the Peruvian Star System. Melvin eyed the menu with his third left eye; the others watched a school of glowing pyerfish pass, their tentacles spindling behind their gelatinous bodies like long strands of snot.

Bob slid his menu into a slot on the side of his enormous rectangular head. The menu stopped, and the scanner started. Bright white light seeped out of Bob's left ear slot, eyes, nose, and mouth before finally spewing out of the right ear slot and dimming. The menu popped through, landing perfectly into Bob's waiting, webbed palm.

"Always too much to choose from," Bob said, but in a language unable to be recorded or understood in any symbols or letters.

"Precisely why I always order the same thing," Melvin responded, in the same unrecordable language.

Over near the bar, a large Cactusaur was causing a commotion. Its eight spiky limbs whisked in every direction. Law enforcers tried cuffing him, each fighting to take a limb or two. Known to be heavy drinkers – with the ability to store enough processed ethanol to stay drunk for a Nimbus Moon cycle or two – this fellow had a particular knack for being nasty when he drank. And he must have been tanked, too, with the way the hologram-tender hovered and cried in the corner.

Their regular waiter, Ronnie, flew over, a small Brandackian with beady, black eyes and slippery, orange skin. His nose and upper lip moved as one, like a walrus in the zoology museum on Sperve where Bob and Melvin met every other Friday. He fluttered on opaque wings centered on his back, which appeared too fragile and tiny to carry his husky frame.

"What can I getcha?" Ronnie asked, his T-shirt too short to cover his plump belly.

"I'll have a bucket of cold mud, side of roach cake," Melvin said while scanning the menu at Flo's Diner, the intergalactic greasy spoon in the middle of the Sid Galaxy.

"Dog soup?" Ronnie asked.

"Hold the hail."

Ronnie faced Bob. "You?"

"I'll start with a shot from the south, put a hat on it, a bloom of breath, two portions of dog and maggot, extra maggot, and...what's your seafood special today?"

"Angels on Horseback."

"Ooh. I hardly knew they were in season. Are those fourth quadrant or planetary?"

"Planetary."

"Perfect. Give me two dozen Angels," Bob said, his tongue lapping his nose hole.

"Make it two, two-dozen," Melvin added his eyes back to the waiter.

Ronnie looked up. "You want forty-eight Angels?"

"Oh, no," Melvin said. "Forty-eight's too many. I want two dozen, and Bob wants two dozen."

"For a total of four dozen, Ronnie. Not forty-eight." Bob smiled.

Ronnie rolled his eyes in a complete circle, the white showing briefly, before he nodded and said, "Right. Four dozen." He flew away, mumbling.

At the bar, the Cactusaur had finally been restrained. Spiky barbs lay scattered like all those needles everyone's looking for in haystacks, except out in the open, and in one huge pile, easy to see on the glass floor without the hay in the way. The law enforcers caught hundreds of barbs in their Evergreen reptilian skin where it wasn't covered by their short sleeved uniforms.

"It'll take hours to clean out all those barbs," Melvin said, worried. He placed his unihand inside his drink and sucked the dark, smoky liquid through the tip of his index finger. "Sure hope nothing bad happens while they're indisposed."

"Nothing bad will happen. Don't worry so much," Bob said, unscrewing the bolts in his neck and lifting off his head. "I'll tell you the ones who have to worry are the enforcers. Those barbs sting like the suns of Peruvia." He put his chalky, bald head onto the base charger he'd brought with him.

"Powering down?" Melvin asked, vapors escaping from his six eyes, which ranged in color from pansy-poppy-pink to walnut-rub-brown.

"No, of course not. I forgot to charge last night. Please don't gas, Melvin. I didn't mean to hurt your feelings."

Melvin's three triangulate smiles connected until the centerplex was a kaleidoscope of pleasure. He dipped his finger into his drink.

The medic crew scrambled in the diner carrying floaters for the wounded law enforcers. A massive Garganticus holding a two-pronger approached the Cactusaur. What remained of the Cactusaur's speckled gray-green skin was blotched with watermelon pink flesh where the barbs had been ripped out. Small stems swelled where there had once been yellow and white flowers.

The Garganticus – wearing a name tag stating *Bill* – rammed the two-pronger tips into the Cactusaur, shocking him into cryosleep. Then, Bill wrapped a bubble sheet around the Cactusaur's spiky body until the barbs were covered. The creature lay encased in a tube of clear poppies, like enormous zits waiting to burst. Bill hefted the tube onto his shoulder, snapping several of the poppies, and carried the offender out of the diner.

"Wonder what that was all about," Melvin said, sounding worried again. "I hope there aren't any more like him around."

"Relax," Bob said. "Nothing ever happens at Flo's Diner. Sure, it's in the bad part of the galaxy, and it's visited by every vagrant species in the universe. Not to overlook the fact that it's in a very secluded portion of the galaxy parcels from the nearest enforcer outpost."

Melvin's mouths were wide; his six eyes wider.

Bob continued. "My point is we meet here every week, and there's never been a problem before. What are the chances there could be two problems in the same day?"

Melvin smiled. "I guess you're right."

A containment crew appeared next with a brown, scaly alien leading the way. He set a square box on the floor beside the barbs, his own hands and face covered in aluminum spandex saran-a-hide protective gear. The box buzzed, unfolded several times, and sprouted out three sets of mechanical legs. It crab walked across the mess, its tipped legs click-clacking above the dull din of the near-empty diner. It was, after all, late afternoon on a Tuesday. The box suddenly screeched into gear, suctioning up each and every barb, leaving a glistening sheen to the floor before it shut off and closed back into its neat square box. The alien gently lifted it and stalked away without a word.

"Here you are," Ronnie said, nearing the table.

He set two bowls of Angels on Horseback in front of both Bob and Melvin. The heat jumping off smelled of salt and sweat. Melvin's unihand hovered over the steam, inhaling deeply. Bob lifted his head from the charger and hung it near Melvin's unihand. The steam fogged Bob's eyes. A machine clicked on, wiping his eyes clear as Bob snapped and locked his head back in place.

Ronnie set the two portions of dog and maggot, the shot from the south with a hat on it, and the bucket of cold mud with roach cake onto the hovering table.

"The dog soup is coming right out. Ran out of two-headed dog, and the cook had to run to the next galaxy to get some more."

"Oh, too bad," Melvin said, his eyes drooping, his skin sagging as he seemed to melt into his seat. "It's very far from here."

"I poured you what was left," Ronnie quickly added. "Not too much, but enough for a taste."

Melvin perked right back up, as if an air pump had filled him. "Really? I—"

"Everybody freeze!"

All eyes – and there were already more than your average number of eyes in the diner considering Melvin had six of his own – stared at the holoport near the entrance where two strange looking creatures had suddenly materialized.

"They match," Melvin exclaimed, petrified. Liquid seeped from a patch of holes at the base of each eye and on his back.

"What the obsidian are they?" Bob whispered to Ronnie, who was high tailing it toward the kitchen and couldn't possibly have heard him. Bob's body slipped beneath the cloth covering the table and collapsed on the clear floor. Melvin slithered beside him, his eyes pods creeping out beneath the tablecloth.

"Nobody move a muscle!" one of the creatures shouted.

"Or I'll spill your guts out," the other said.

The first one was smaller framed than the second one, with tendrils falling from the top of its head on its backside. Bob wondered if it was strips of skin, or fur, or perhaps grass, but with no knowledge of the species, it was pure speculation. The other had short fur, or skin strips, or grass, which clumped on the top of its head. Bob thought maybe the stuff was detachable and had the strongest urge to reach out and test his theory. What scared Bob the most were the faces of these two creatures. They were symmetrical. What purpose could there ever be to have two equally set eyes above a centered nose and mouth?

"They're hideous," Melvin whispered.

"I know." Bob cringed.

"What sort of a god would create something as horrible as those?"

Bob didn't know.

"What are they?" Melvin asked.

"I'm not sure. I'm searching the universal web right now." Bob's eyes swiveled in his head as whirring noises spouted from his throat.

The creatures held long black weapons in their two matching hands, stood upright on two matching legs, and Bob thought if they were sliced from top to bottom, they would form two perfect halves of...whatever they were.

"Yup. As I thought," Bob said.

"What?" Melvin cringed.

"Humans. The long haired one is a female, the other is the male."

Melvin stared, all six eyes spreading out to catch different angles. "How can we understand them?"

"It's a primitive form of clicks and grunts; easy to grasp. The mind wraps around its simplicity and translates the fuller, more complex definition."

"Really?" Melvin said, impressed.

"No, they are wearing voice boxes. See."

Melvin stared at the black boxes with silver mesh screens strapped around the human's throats. "Do they eat septoptics?" Melvin asked, worried.

"Hang on." Bob searched, his eyes twitching. "Doesn't look like it."

Melvin sighed.

The humans – who by now Melvin and Bob had learned were You Idiot (the male) and Ice Queen (though the female looked nothing like royalty) – walked around the room from table to table. Their skin was black and shiny, slippery to the touch if either Bob or Melvin had ventured close enough to find out. The color changed to a pale matte orange at the hands. The texture became gritty over their toeless feet.

"This is a bloody robbery!" the female belted. She aimed her black weapon at the ceiling and shot a hot white light into the air.

"Way to go, Ice Queen. Why don't you shoot a hole in the wall so the entire place will cave in," You Idiot said.

"Shut up, you idiot!"

"Toss all your valuables on the floor in front of you," You Idiot said, waving the tip of his fire stick around the diner.

Melvin focused one eye on Bob. "What's *valuables*?"

Bob shrugged. "I haven't the foggiest."

"I wished you'd never said that."

"What?"

"That nothing ever happens at Flo's Diner on a Tuesday."

Bob gulped hard.

They watched You Idiot and the Ice Queen move about collecting said valuables from the patrons who hid beneath the tables: a bag of stardust, a Laridian Almanac, a spool of gold thread, two tickets to the Intergalactic Reunion Tour of the New Squids on the Rock.

"They can't be valuable," Melvin said, pointing at the tickets, "even to a human."

Bob nodded.

If any alien did not provide You Idiot or the Ice Queen with their valuables, then You Idiot would yank the creature out, which was awkward and a bit embarrassing for everyone when the mucous membrane called Snivel came up empty-handed. Then, they would point their fire sticks into what Bob assumed they thought to be a vulnerable spot. Once, the Ice Queen grabbed a Tinktataur by the balls and slipped the fire stick into the crook of its elbow joint covered in a cast of Marsconium, which everybody knows is unbreakable. The ball squeeze seemed to hurt the poor guy the most, although she didn't make the connection. The human males' anatomy seemed quite different from a Tinktataur, according to the diagram on galactipedia.

Melvin shuddered. "They don't know what they're doing! Should we try to attack them?"

"How?"

"I don't know. You're the one with two synthetic brains."

"I wouldn't know where to start. Just because I have these brains doesn't mean I have your courage."

Melvin smiled, all three smiles. "You're my best friend."

"I know."

"You!" the Ice Queen screeched, kicking her boot beneath the tablecloth.

"Interesting," Bob muttered.

"What?" Melvin asked, panicked.

"I read humans have five digits on each foot while this female has none."

"What does it mean?" Melvin asked eyes wide except for the one still peering at the Ice Queen from beneath the tablecloth.

"Nothing, most likely. Could be a human anomaly. I don't know enough about the species. Judging by these two, it's no wonder they are such a loathed life form. Barely able to walk on two legs, yet trying to take over the galaxy."

Melvin bellowed sound waves as the Ice Queen dragged him from beneath the table by his lingering eye pod. You Idiot shoved his fire stick into the side of Melvin's head. Melvin let out a gas bubble to rival the Big Bang gases of creation.

"Dear God!" the Ice Queen said, covering her mouth and nose with her hand.

You Idiot clicked a button on his fire stick. Bob heard the flame power up. Melvin's six eyes dripped oily tears into a growing puddle beneath him.

"Give me your valuables," the Ice Queen shouted.

"I...have....none," Melvin stuttered.

"Are you crying...oil?" You Idiot asked, pointing to Melvin's tears.

Melvin cried louder, his three mouths merging into one wailing, black hole. You Idiot jabbed the fire stick into Melvin's head, which pressed in and slowly popped back out like one of those peanut shaped candies Bob remembered having as a kid.

"Stop your blubbering," You Idiot said, "or I'll disintegrate you."

This, of course, sent Melvin into hysterics, shrieking and blubbering harder, pouring black oil all over himself, the Ice Queen, and You Idiot. The humans' faces contorted, and Bob knew he was seconds away from watching his best friend of over three-hundred Peruvian sun cycles become a crispified pile of ash on the floor of Flo's Diner. What was the matter with these humans? Didn't they know it was Tuesday?

It happened so fast.

You Idiot stumbled, slipping on the slick oil of Melvin's tears. His fire stick swung around, nailing the Ice Queen in the side of the head and knocking her to the ground. Red liquid poured out of her head holes, and her bone structure appeared compromised where the fire stick had smashed. Bob had the feeling her cavity was abandoned, and wondered where human souls drifted when their bodies were used up.

As the fire stick swung back around, already primed and loaded, You Idiot grabbed a hold of Melvin and yanked him down by several eyes, like grabbing the strings of balloons. They toppled over, twisting and tangling, rolling in Melvin's oily tears as You Idiot's finger twitched and clicked the fire stick's 'on' button.

"No!" Bob screamed, as his auto-defense gel secreted and suctioned to his body.

Melvin's six eyes held Bob's gaze as he, the Ice Queen, and You Idiot exploded in a bluish orange flame tipped in neon green. The force from the blast sucked everything in, and then propelled it outward in a nanosecond. Everything was destroyed: the patrons, the bar, Ronnie, the Angels on Horseback Melvin would never eat, plus the glass floors and walls of Flo's Intergalactic Diner and Bar. Everything, vaporized. Including the Ice Queen and You Idiot, who never did get to take any of those valuables.

Why would they do this? And on a Tuesday, when the universe was a safe place? When two portions of dog and maggot was enough? When Melvin and Bob traveled a light year to enjoy lunch, Peruvian pyerfish, and each other's company?

But not this Tuesday.

On this Tuesday, Bob watched his best friend die, and he was too cowardly to stop it.

"Need a lift?"

Bob turned. A Speickel Taxi hovered in the air behind him. Had he called a taxi?

"I was in the area," the driver said. He was a Foomanchuian with dark skin covered in chocolate colored fur that spread out from the top of his head and curved straight down his sides. "What happened here?"

"A hold up," Bob said, stepping into the taxi. "Humans."

"Jeesh. Looks bad. You all right?"

Bob stared at the empty space that used to be Flo's. Pieces of shrapnel spun aimlessly, still stuck in the artificial gravity.

"No. But, I'll be fine."

"Where to?"

Where to? A very interesting question. Bob needed answers. What could life be like on Earth to make its inhabitants need these valuables? They were monsters, these humans. They should be exterminated. The galaxy was not safe as long as Earth existed. And there was only one being with the power to make it happen. "Take me to *The Capital*."

"On Planet 9?"

Bob didn't answer. He closed his eyes as the taxi driver toggled the remote and slipped coordinates onto the touch screen. Bob pressed the knob on the side of his neck. The whirring in his head slowed as he initiated his shut down. The last thing he heard was the slurred voice of the driver telling him it would be a short flight to Planet 9.

* * *

When Bob rebooted, they were docking in the central parking garage of Planet 9.

"Your total's forty-five parsnips," the Foomanchuian said.

Bob reached for his money clip, handed the driver a fifty, and said, "Thanks a lot. I don't know what I would have done if you hadn't showed up."

The driver smiled, his hair spreading out like freshly mown grass. "If you need me again, just call." He handed Bob his business card, a piece of Plexiglas with hypermorphic circuits running throughout to light up the driver's name and number.

"I will," Bob said, knowing good and well he would *never* call the number or see the cabbie again.

He scuttled along the metallic flooring of the garage's downward spiraling ramp. After a while, he reached his level and stepped outside, noticing the gloom of the overcast sky mirrored the computer-generated garage ceiling. The buildings loomed across the skyline reminding Bob of the long-stemmed eye pod eyes belonging to Melvin.

A large sign staked in the concrete outside of a short wooden shack read *The Capital.* Bob looked over the deserted city street. His gaze returned to the dilapidated organic structure wedged between the most brilliant architecture known in the galaxy, at least in the *known* galaxy.

With a shrug, Bob reached out for the ball in the door's center, a 'knob' he recalled from the history show he enjoyed watching. "What an old-fashioned contraption," he snorted, turning it with his webbed hand and pushing the plank inward. The door creaked on rusty hinges, and when he closed it behind him, the musty room turned black. Bob clicked his teeth and bright light shot out from his eyes. A variety of knick-knacks covered the walls, from Clyzakian coon tails to bonefish from the Trianon Sea. Parchments encased in wooden boxes covered in dirty glass contained porcelain Brandackian and Cactasaur dolls. Who would want to collect those, Bob couldn't imagine. Although he had never been in *The Capital* building, somehow his expectations were way off.

"Can I help ya?"

Bob swiveled his head, his high beams finding the face of the voice who spoke to him. The face had no features. The body was a horizontal slab with two limbs attached to it.

"Tarnations, son," the creature spoke. "Think ya could point them shiners elsewhere?"

"Oh!" Bob answered, embarrassed. "My apologies. It was too dark to see, and these beams are light sensitive. I'll override my system." He clicked his lights to low, which diffused the spreading ray. Wood shavings blanketed the bare floor, accounting for the scent of mildew and sawdust.

The creature came back into the light. He appeared to be more like a house on stilts. "Now," the creature said, "what can I do ya for?"

"I need to speak to the Emissary."

"The Consigliore?"

"The President."

"Oh, His Greatness."

Bob huffed. "Whatever he goes by, I need to speak with him."

The creature entered a metamorphosis. Its limbs doubled, fattened up, and lowered while the horizontal slab turned vertical and widened. A bulbous top pushed up sprouting hair on one side and a face on the other. Bob gasped in horror as the creature grew two eyes, one nose, and one mouth stacked in perfect symmetry.

"I am His Greatness."

Bob's mouth hung wide. "You're a—human!"

"Ain't I?" the creature asked. "Ain't that what ya see?"

"I don't understand," Bob said, his systems speeding up. "What is happening today? Tuesday is supposed to be the most non-eventful day of the week, but my diner explodes, my best friend disintegrates, and now, I'm finding out a human runs all of Planet 9! Is nothing sacred?"

Bob was panting, his entire being drenched in a gummy material which secreted in pulsing waves from holes in his body.

"Here," said His Greatness, handing him a square cloth.

"Thank you," Bob said, regaining his composure. "You'll have to forgive me. It's been a busy day."

His Greatness leaned forward against the counter, eyes twinkling a deep shade of blue. "Can I tell ya a secret?"

Bob sniffled.

"They don't all got evil in 'em, *humans*, I mean."

Bob looked up. "Are you trying to make me feel better?"

His Greatness shrugged. "Maybe. I know somethin' that'll tickle your pickle and make ya smile. How's about thinkin' you and your friend was in the wrong place at the wrong time, and nothin' more?"

Bob thought about the time he had been stranded on Planet Meridian where he met Yolanda, an exotic yodeler from the Meridian Alps. They had spent an entire evening yodeling and romping on the snowy beaches beneath the twin moons. Now *that* thought made him feel better. This one? Not so much.

"What if," His Greatness said, "ya could slip back to before the humans liquefied yar friend? Would ya change much?"

"Why, I'd save Melvin, of course."

"Well, bobble my head, son. Ain't ya forgettin' the others? Wouldn't leavin' them behind be like pullin' the trigger yarself? Might as well have taken them valuables, too, while yar at it."

"How do you know all this?"

"I'm His Greatness, the ruler of all."

Bob's nostril flared. "Are you God?"

"Nah, but I work for him." He winked. "I'm what you're needin' and not a thing more. But, you ain't answered my question still. Wouldn't ya be as guilty as a two-headed dog stealin' bovine cutlets off the front porch if'n you'd left all them creatures behind? Why, you'd be to blame as much as them thievin' humans if'n ya—"

"Those humans came there to hurt everyone!"

"Did they, now?" His Greatness asked, placing a white stick into his perfectly round mouth and setting the stick on fire.

The sight of the fire choked Bob up. What had actually happened in the diner? He replayed the footage he'd recorded earlier. He scrutinized the humans. They had weapons to destroy, but they hadn't harmed anyone. The damage occurred when You Idiot's finger slipped, and his fire stick ignited Melvin's flammable tears.

"Are you saying it was an accident?"

"Wasn't it?" His Greatness said, puffing out gray clouds of smoke.

Bob shook his head. "What they did was wrong, and if they hadn't been breaking the law, Melvin would still be alive."

"Along with all them others."

"Yes, I suppose you're right."

"Well, slap my cheeks and call me Sally, son. What ya waitin' fer?"

His Greatness blew out a dense cloud of dark smoke, saturating Bob, who hacked and coughed as his lungs filled with the mess. As the smoke cleared, Bob lifted his head. He was in the cab again. The Fumanchuian was driving.

"He awakens," the driver said.

"What am I doing here?"

"You're on your way to Flo's Intergalactic Diner and Bar. It's Tuesday, Bob. You always meet Melvin there on Tuesday."

"It's Tuesday?" Bob whispered, scratching the insides of his ear holes. He bolted upright. "Did you say *meet Melvin*?"

"Of course. That's what you told me."

"Never mind what I told you," Bob said quickly. "Where's Melvin? Do you know him?"

"Of course I do. Jeesh, Bob. You need to power up longer before you go out. You're sounding cuckoo."

"Never mind. Take me to Melvin."

"Whatever you say, buddy."

They pulled into Flo's with a screech of tires on the floating tar pavement outside the diner. Bob jumped out of the cab, and said, "Keep it idling. I'll be right back."

"But, its Tuesday," he heard the Fumanchian chime out as he jogged away from the cab.

Melvin sat at their usual table, the floater in the glass bubble with the view of the Peruvian Star System. He was eyeing the menu with his third left eye, the others watching a school of glowing pyerfish pass, their tentacles spindling behind their gelatinous bodies like long strands of snot.

"Melvin," Bob said under his breath. He crossed the diner and slid into the empty seat at the table.

"Hey, Bob," Melvin said. "What took you so long?"

"A lot's happened today. Come on, let's get out of here."

Melvin's eyes all swiveled over to stare at Bob. "But, it's Tuesday."

Bob shrugged, standing. "I know, but sometimes you have to shake life up a bit."

"You feeling all right?"

A large Cactusaur was causing a commotion near the bar, whisking eight spiky limbs in every direction as the law enforcers tried cuffing him, each taking a limb or two.

Bob knew exactly what he needed to do. "Give me a sec, Melvin. I'll be right back."

Bob shimmied over to the law enforcers and pulled one aside. He explained how humans were coming to steal all the valuables – which he had to explain more than once – and someone needed to be there to help save everyone. But, the law enforcer wouldn't listen. Bob couldn't blame him, though he pleaded.

When he rushed back to the table, Ronnie was waiting to take their order. "Not now, Ronnie," Bob said, turning to Melvin. "I don't know how to explain this, but any minute two humans are going to show up and try to rob the place."

"Humans?" Melvin said, his swiveling eye pods searching for the threat. "How can you be sure?"

"There's no time to explain. I need you to trust me."

Melvin's third left eye pulled in to stare at Bob. "Of course I trust you. I trust you with my life."

Bob shivered. A moment later, the Ice Queen and You Idiot materialized in the holoport. Melvin's life *did* depend on him. "Stay put," Bob told Melvin.

"What are you going to do?" Melvin asked as Bob walked away.

"Make everything right," he replied.

The humans' backs faced him as he approached. He gently tapped You Idiot's shoulder, who swung around, apparently surprised by Bob's manners. Perhaps humans always entered rooms shouting on Earth. He'd have to look it up later.

"What the hell are you doing?" You Idiot screeched.

"Pardon me, Mr. Idiot, but I'm afraid you are not welcome here."

"Shoot him in the face," Ice Queen shouted.

Slowly, Bob stood; his torso unfolded, his shoulders straightened, his neck stretched until he reached his full height towering over the humans. The Ice Queen and You Idiot bent back as their necks craned.

"Dear God," the Ice Queen said, which Bob found to be strange. Praying, now?

"It's freaking Frankenstein." You Idiot wiped liquid from his forehead, and Bob couldn't help but think how disgusting and inappropriate for the man to relieve himself out in the open. And right above his mouth! Eww! Bob hoped the human species used another orifice for eating. He'd have to look that up later, too.

"Stay back," You Idiot shouted, as he grabbed Melvin, who had not listened, and used his body for a shield, "or this one dies."

"Not likely," Bob said, reaching out for You Idiot's fire stick with his enormous six-fingered palm, and noticing, for the first time, it was double the size of You Idiot's head. He grasped the fire stick by the handle, heating up the coils in his webbed hand, and watched as it became too hot for the human to hold.

"Jesus Christ, it's hot," You Idiot said, shaking his blistered palm.

"The name's Bob. I'm sure you've mistaken me for someone else."

A loud *crack* filled the air as the Ice Queen readied her fire stick, aiming it at Bob. "You've screwed with the wrong woman."

"My apologies, Your Highness."

"See," You Idiot blurted, "even this alien knows you're an ice queen."

Bob turned, taking in the room around him as time dropped to a Snail Parcel for everyone but him. The Ice Queen's lips moved slowly as she shouted expletives at You Idiot. Patrons cowered beneath tables and chairs. The staff of Flo's hid behind the kitchen wall, spying through the opening leading to the cook station. Ronnie was on the caller to the law enforcers, who Bob knew were unavailable, as they were undergoing seventy-two hour barb removal therapy.

They were all the same. They wanted to survive. And although he didn't know the reasons behind the Ice Queen and You Idiot's hold up, he figured they didn't want to die either. But, he wasn't about to wait and find out.

While the humans argued about the Ice Queen's royal status – which made no sense to Bob at all – he took advantage of the situation and brightened his eyes, shooting out blinding light. As he did, the humans covered their faces, and he grabbed the other fire stick. But not before one of them went off.

The blast entered Bob's midsection and exited out his rear, leaving behind a gaping hole. His particles poured out too quickly for his metabolic systems to rebuild. Melvin knelt beside him, oily tears filling his eyes. Bob scanned the diner for the humans. He couldn't let this have all been in vain. If Melvin seeped oil and the fire sticks went off...

No. The humans were laid up. The Foomanchuian held them down while Ronnie clamped their hands together with wire. It should hold them till someone could come take them to the nearest moon prison. Thank God for the cabbie! Melvin was saved. The diner was saved. Bob, not so much. But, he didn't care.

"I'm dying," Bob said, looking up with a pained smile.

Melvin shook his head, his eye pods scanning Bob's body for a way to help.

"I want you to power me down," Bob said. "Take out my life chip and keep it. It contains everything I know, every memory and dream, and I want you to have it."

Melvin smiled sadly, vapors and oil seeping from his eyes. "Okay, Bob. I will."

"Never let go, Melvin."

"But, I'm not holding you—"

"Promise me!" Bob shouted.

"I'll never let go," Melvin stuttered through tears, and he reached up behind Bob's ear and powered him down.

***

A bright white light shown in the distance, and Bob couldn't help but want to move toward it. His name was being called. This must be the afterlife. Oh well, at least Melvin had survived. But, it was Melvin's voice which he heard calling his name. Oh dirt! He hadn't made it either. Well, this hadn't worked out the way Bob had hoped. Suddenly, his eyes shot open.

"Bob, you're awake."

Melvin sat beside Bob in a hospital room. Bob looked around, and then lifted the sheet to make sure his body was still intact. It was. "What happened?"

Melvin snorted. "What happened is a miracle. You were leaking out, and I powered you down, like you told me to. But, you'd also told me to never let go, so I couldn't leave to get help. Finally, the Fumanchuian helped me carry you to his cab, after the humans were put in the cooler till law enforcers could come. Then we drove across the galaxy and got stuck in traffic. It was googleplex-hour traffic."

"On the Hitchhiker's Highway?"

"Yes."

"Rough."

"I know. Anyway, after a week, we exited and went straight to Planet 9 to meet the Emissary."

"The Consigliore?"

"The President."

"Oh, His Greatness."

"Yes," Melvin said. "His Greatness. And how great he is. Did you know he's a human?"

"I did."

"He's nothing like the ones who held up the diner. They were criminals who had escaped Earth prison and started robbing diners along the highway. Y'know, places like Flo's right off the main road and not in the nicest parts of the galaxy."

Bob didn't answer.

"He was able to fix you right up. Gave you a new core, but enabled your old life chip." Melvin swiveled an eye across Bob's chart along the wall. "They say you can leave today. Isn't it great news?"

"It sure is. I'd like to go see His Greatness...say thank you."

"Of course. We should call a cab."

"Check my pant pockets. I should have the Fumanchuian's card. Never thought I'd need it, though." As Melvin searched for the card, Bob asked, "What day is it?"

"It's Tuesday. Why?"

"I was thinking maybe after we visit *The Capital* we could go have lunch."

"At Flo's?"

Bob smiled. "Life's short. Let's try a new joint this time."

AT THE CROSSROADS

A light snow was falling as Charlie Reardon left the diner and made his way down Madison Street. He shivered in the November air, pushing bare hands deeper into stretched overcoat pockets. Gray eyes bore ahead protected from the elements by the brim of a well-worn fedora.

"Hey, Chuck. You looking for some company?"

Charlie passed Doris, numb to her charm. Her blonde hair curled from beneath a Russian fur hat like down; her full-length minx hid long legs he knew too well.

"Not tonight, Doris."

She pressed over to him, her four-inch heels tapping across the pavement, and linked arms. "What's the matter, baby? Don't you want me to keep you warm?"

"No," Charlie said, shaking free. "I said not tonight."

"Suit yourself," Doris said, swinging curved hips as she shimmied away.

Charlie crossed the street, casting an eye over his shoulder as a black car screeched to a spot at the opposite curb. Doris leaned in against the door frame.

A deal was struck. And she slipped into the car and out of sight. Charlie sighed.

Maybe I should have said yes.

He turned from Madison onto Lincoln reaching the precinct as the snow started falling in heavy drifts. Shaking off his coat and hat, Charlie crossed to his desk in the center of the homicide department. A note scribbled in the secretary's ink on yellow legal paper sat on top of his stacked files:

Susan called –Urgent!
on 11/18/48, at 9:28 p.m.

Charlie noted June's precision. No one else would include the date, especially not the year, but June. He figured it had to do with being named after a month, kind of connected her to the calendar. Charlie picked up the telephone.

"Good evening, Northeast Nebraska Telephone Company," the switchboard operator said.

"Could I be connected to Susan Reynolds in Hartington?"

"One moment, please."

After a few hollow clicks, the line connected.

"Hello?"

Her cloudy voice brought back memories.

"Susan, it's Charlie. Is everything okay?"

Even after six years, he still worried too much.

"Fine. Just cold."

"Your message said it was urgent." He tapped a pencil on his files.

"The boiler's out again. And the snow's picked up. I think we're in for a big one."

Charlie rubbed his temples, his elbow resting on his desk. "You check the coal level? Maybe it's out."

"The coal's fine," she said. "I could really use your help."

Charlie checked his watch. 9:38 p.m. What a way to start his shift. "All right, Susan. I'll see what I can do."

"Thanks, Charlie. The wind's really picked up. Be careful out there."

"Sure, Susan." He hung up and stepped to the window. The wind pushed the trees in unnatural angles. "Sure wish I didn't have to go out in this."

"No such luck, Chuck."

Charlie turned. Sam Duncan held out a cup of coffee. "Whatcha got?" Charlie asked, taking the coffee from him. He took a sip and grimaced. He'd think Sam would remember he took his coffee with sugar by now, but it was the thought that counted.

"A passerby spotted a Buick parked on the curb off Roosevelt, the Madison end. Said it looked suspicious."

"Why's that?"

"Something about the angle it was parked at."

Charlie faced the window. "Sam, it's really coming down. Plus I promised Susan I'd stop by and take a look at her boiler."

"Is it busted again?"

"I don't know. Maybe. Probably just something minor. Can the car wait 'til later?"

Sam grabbed his keys from his desk and put on his jacket. "Tell you what, partner. I'll give you a ride to Susan's so you don't have to walk."

"Thanks, Sam."

"After, we have a look at this suspicious vehicle."

"Fair enough," Charlie said, throwing up his hands in surrender. He slid back into his coat and hat, worn and fitted like a second skin. "It's gonna be a long night."

The wind gusted. Snow fell hard with an inch already covering the ground. Roosevelt Drive, located a few short blocks away, took much longer to reach in the storm.

The black Buick with equally dark tinted windows had no tag – the second suspicious thing Charlie noticed, the first being the passenger tires, both of which were on the curb.

"That's an odd way to park," Sam said. He peered in through the front windshield.

Charlie pulled the driver's side door handle. Locked. He glimpsed in the window, then pressed his face to the glass for a closer look.

"Charlie."

Charlie looked up. Sam was pointing down into the passenger side. Charlie nodded, drawing his gun and clicking the safety off as he met Sam on the sidewalk. With his eyes, Sam motioned the countdown and on three, flung the door open. Charlie aimed at whoever was inside the car. Immediately, he brought down his weapon, his heart dead weight in his chest.

"Radio the precinct," Charlie said. "We've got a homicide."

A team of officers quickly arrived and taped off the area. Forensics dusted for fingerprints. The coroner declared it an official homicide at 10:52 p.m. A crowd gathered, not caring that the weather was worsening, the snow thickening to a gray gloom.

"Nothing to see here," Charlie said, waving them off like flies. "Go back about your business."

A reporter from the Nebraska Gazette snapped a picture, the flash nearly blinding Charlie.

"What's your problem, buddy?" Charlie asked, his blanched eyes seeing hot white.

"I don't have a problem. Just doing my job. Why don't you go do the same, *buddy*?"

"Why, you son of a…"

Sam grabbed Charlie by the collar and swung him away. "Cool down," he said. "Let me deal with this guy."

Charlie reached the sidewalk just as Sergeant Riley ducked beneath the crime tape. He stood over six-feet tall, wiry, with thin graying hair and sunken cheeks, a sharp contrast against Charlie's muscular, one-hundred and seventy-five pound frame and black, crew-cut hair.

"Who's the girl?" Riley asked.

The woman lying dead across the backseat looked no older then twenty with short blonde hair in tattered curls and eyes like a blue sky behind thick clouds. Her blouse lay opened revealing an ample chest covered in blood from the fatal knife wounds.

Charlie glanced away, taking a step back.

"Her name's Doris Lane," Stan Watson said. A squirrelly fellow, he wore horn-rimmed glasses, and kept his moustache perfectly manicured. "She lives on Baker Street. Works for Kirt Madson."

Riley's eyebrows arched. "A call girl?"

"Yes. And not one who's been in trouble before. She kept to herself, stayed to her business. Just looks like she got in the wrong car."

Charlie remembered Doris slipping into the black Buick, wishing he'd caught a good look of the driver. At the time, he didn't know he needed to. He couldn't tell the Sergeant he'd employed Doris's services on a steady basis. It would cost him his job. Now he wished he'd said 'yes' to her and taken her back to his place. He could've called in sick and no one would've been the wiser. Then she'd be lying in his bed keeping him warm instead of lying cold in the backseat of a parked car.

"Well, get her to the morgue. Hopefully an autopsy will shed some light on who did this." Riley shivered. "Doesn't look like this storm is gonna let up tonight. See you boy's back at the station."

"Take it easy, Sarge," Charlie said, the weight in his chest compressing his lungs. In the shadows of the storefronts, a figure crossed between the buildings and down an alleyway. Charlie's instinct told him to follow. He caught Sam's attention.

"What's up?" Sam asked.

"I think I saw someone," Charlie said. They drew their guns before turning down the alley.

Up ahead, someone rounded the corner. "FREEZE!" Charlie said, sprinting forward. "NNPD!" Out of breath, he dashed around the corner where he and Sam found the guy cornered with his back to a brick wall.

The man raised his hands. "Now, officers. I don't mean any trouble."

With their weapons locked, the detectives approached the suspect cautiously. "Oh yeah, pal. Then what made ya run?" Sam said.

"A copper yells freeze. What am I suppose t'do?"

Motioning with his gun, Charlie said, "Step aside, into the light. Keep you hands up. I wanna see your face."

The suspect did as he was told. The streetlight illuminated his face. "You're just a kid," Sam said. "What are ya, fifteen?"

"Sixteen," the kid said.

"Whaddaya doin' out here, kid?" Charlie asked, lowering his weapon.

"I got a message for Detective Charlie Reardon," he said, showing a folded square of paper in his palm that had gone unnoticed.

"You can give that to me," Charlie said. "I'll take care of it."

"Who'd ya get it from?" Sam said.

The kid shrugged. "Some guy. He told me he'd give me five bucks up front to deliver that message to Detective Charlie Reardon near Madison off Roosevelt around eleven. When I saw all the coppers, I got scared. Real scared. So I ran."

"A young woman's been murdered," Charlie said. "And I'd bet whoever sent you here had something to do with it."

"Murdered?" the kid repeated, his eyes wide.

"You're gonna need to go with Detective Duncan to make your statement."

"Son," Sam said to the kid. He didn't respond, his face bleached under the lights. "Son?" The kid turned pale, wet eyes his way. "You remember what the guy looked like?" The kid nodded. "Come with me," Sam said, leading the boy down the alley.

Charlie opened the paper and read the message. He broke into a cold sweat. "What the hell?" He stumbled out of the alley where Sam met him on the sidewalk.

"What's wrong with you?" Sam said. "You look like you've seen a ghost."

"Where's the kid?"

"Sarge took him. You all right, Chuck? You don't look so good."

"I need to talk with Kirt Madson." He pressed past Sam to the patrol car.

"Madson?" Sam said, jogging to keep up. "You think Madson's got something to do with the girl's murder?"

"I don't know yet. But he's the closest connection to Doris we've got right now. Worth a shot." He opened his door and sat down. The snow wasn't letting up. Neither was the wind. Sam got in the car and shivered. "What about Susan?"

Charlie closed his eyes and leaned his head against the rest. He'd forgotten about Susan.

"The temperature's dropping fast," Sam said. "If that boiler's out completely—"

"We'll go to Susan's first. It shouldn't take long."

Sam wiped the windshield with his sleeve. "Can you believe this weather?"

Charlie stared out the window, the piece of paper scrunched in his fist.

He didn't know what to believe.

****

Fifteen minutes later, they pulled into Susan's driveway. The lights were off and the house looked abandoned. Sam killed the engine.

"She was expecting you, wasn't she?" Sam asked.

"*She* called me." Charlie lifted his gun.

"What are you doing?"

"Susan always leaves a light on."

The detectives leapt out of the car through the thick snow and heavy winds, up the porch steps to the front door. Sam motioned the plan and on three, kicked the door open. They rushed in, covering each other as they moved from room to room in near blackness.

"Susan!" Charlie called.

No answer.

"She's not here," Sam said. "Check the basement."

They stepped through the country kitchen to the basement door. Sam flipped the light switch.

Nothing.

"Lights are out," Sam said.

Charlie opened the cabinet beneath the sink hoping Susan still kept her flashlights there. He grabbed one and turned it on. A stream of light flared in a circle against the far wall.

Charlie flung open the basement door and aimed the light down the staircase. "Susan?" he called. He descended the stairs, shining the beam around the room with Sam close behind.

"Susan?" Charlie called. "You down here?"

No answer.

Then, Charlie saw her bare feet. Her butchered chest. Her lifeless body. He froze.

"Oh, my God," Sam said, pushing past. He crossed the basement to the string hanging from the bulb in the ceiling. With a click, light filled the room, and a hum sliced through the silence. "Charlie. Radio the station."

****

Charlie waited on the front porch steps while for the second time that night the forensics team collected evidence. The wind howled, snow falling in torrents. The wool blanket helped, but the storm was no match for the cold he felt inside.

Sam sat down beside him without a word. What was there to say?

Sergeant Riley ambled toward the house, his trench coat hanging off his lanky frame. "Charlie, I'm so sorry. I know things with you and Susan were difficult, but—" His voice drifted like the snow. "Sam, why don't you take Charlie home? I'll stay here and finish things up."

"Sure thing, Sarge."

"I'm fine," Charlie lied. "I don't need to go home."

"Yes, you do, Charlie. And you will. Come back in the morning. You're no use to any of us right now."

Charlie surrendered, knowing there was no point arguing.

"Now get outta here," Sergeant Riley said, climbing the steps and disappearing into the house.

"Let's get you home," Sam said.

"Not until I talk to Madson."

****

Kirt Madson was a man with striking features. Jet black hair slicked like oil, a set of pearly whites, and green eyes like two pieces of jade. His business flirted on illegal, but Madson remained a pro at keeping his nose clean. His girls were beautiful—movie star beautiful. They knew the rules and rarely got into trouble.

The secluded mansion at the dead end of Pine Drive was encompassed by a wrought iron gate. Sam pulled up and rang the buzzer. A colored man exited the gate house, his uniform pristine, more like a tuxedo than work attire.

"Good evening, detectives," he said, clasping gloved hands near his waist. "May I help you?"

"We'd like to speak with Mr. Madson," Sam said.

"Mr. Madson does not usually take callers at such a late hour. May I ask what the pressing matter at hand is?"

Charlie leaned toward Sam. "It has to do with Doris Lane. I believe she's an employee of Mr. Madson's. We need to ask him a few questions."

"Can't this wait until morning, detective…"

"Reardon. Charlie Reardon, and no, it can't wait. If Mr. Madson prefers, we could bring him down to the station, make it more official?"

The guard stared. "I see. Please wait while I ring the house." He disappeared inside the gatehouse.

Sam turned. "What was that all about?"

"I don't know. I guess Madson needs his beauty rest."

The guard reappeared in the doorway of the gatehouse. He gestured the detectives forward as the massive gates swung open, like two arms seeming to welcome them in; the gears creaked sinisterly. The manicured lawn surrounding the driveway led up to a large fountain around which the paved driveway circled. They parked and both detectives stepped out into the growing storm. They climbed the stairs guarded by massive stone lions on either side and Charlie knocked on the brass knocker and waited.

The large door opened on well-oiled hinges. Kirt Madson stood in the doorway wearing a paisley bathrobe and palming a glass of brandy.

"Detective Reardon, Detective Duncan," he said. "To what do I owe the unexpected pleasure of your company?"

"Aren't you gonna invite us in?" Charlie asked.

"Of course," Madson said, moving aside. "Won't you come in?"

Charlie and Sam stepped onto the Persian rug in the foyer. The double stairs ahead wound up to a balcony hallway where a few of Madson's girls stood watching.

"Not a bad view," Madson said, eyeing his merchandise. Charlie's teeth clenched. "Gentlemen, please. Take off your coats and hats."

Charlie and Sam hung their damp garments on the brass rack near the door. They followed Madson down the narrow hall, passing a bouquet in a large, glass vase like a suspended firework. He led to a dark sitting room with Tiffany lamps and an extensive library. Furniture from different parts of the world decorated the room alongside tapestries and curtains spanning from ceiling to floor like a woman's gown.

"Have a seat," Madson said, sitting in a plush, high back chair. The detectives sat across from him on the loveseat. A hot fire crackled in the fireplace. "Would you care for a cigar?" Madson asked, presenting an opened cedar box packed with expensive Cubans.

Charlie waved him off while Sam dug in with his

pudgy fingers. "Don't mind if I do," Sam said. "Thank you."

Madson handed Sam a matchbook. Charlie tapped his fingers on the arm of the couch.

"Mr. Madson," Charlie said. "Do you employ Doris Lane?"

"Yes," Madson said, puffing his cigar. "Doris is one of my best girls."

"I'm sure that means a lot coming from a guy of your stature," Charlie said, crossing his leg and straightening the pant cuff.

"A man of my stature? I'm sure I don't know quite what you mean, Detective Reardon," he said, exhaling a puff of gray smoke. "My girls are well taken care of. I consider them more like daughters than employees."

"But you have no problem taking your cut."

"It is still a business, no matter what my feelings are for my employees."

"And what about your feelings toward Doris?"

"I already told you: Doris is one of my best girls."

"Doris Lane was found murdered," Sam said.

"Oh my God!" Madson said. "Do you know what happened?"

"Someone stabbed her to death in the chest and left her in a car with no tags."

He shook his head. "Doris was always picking the wrong guys," Madson said, eyeballing Charlie.

Charlie stared back, trying to read Madson's secrets.

"You had no idea?" Sam said.

"None at all."

"Do you know of anyone who would have wanted Doris dead?" Charlie said.

"No one. She was a sweet girl. Had a charming way about her and got along with everyone." He stared off wrapped in his own thoughts.

They sat in awkward silence like the skin of a pudding. Finally, Sam broke it. "Do you know a kid named Tommy Nescott? About sixteen?"

"Nescott? No, I'm afraid his name doesn't ring a bell. Why? Is he a suspect?"

"At the time, no," Sam said.

"Well, I do hope you will keep me updated on the progression of this case." He stood, and Charlie and Sam mirrored. "If there's anything else I can do to help, please don't hesitate to ask. But for the time being, it's very late and I'd like to see you both to the door."

Charlie zeroed in on Madson's eyes as he stood. They seemed to falter for the smallest part of a second, though his smile and mannerisms didn't miss a beat. Was he hiding something? Or genuinely upset about the news? Charlie couldn't read which.

"I'm sorry I wasn't much help," Madson said, when they reached the foyer.

"We appreciate you seeing us so late," Sam said, slipping into his coat and hat.

Charlie tilted his fedora into place and opened the door. Turning, he said, "I wouldn't make any plans to leave town in the next few days until after our investigation is wrapped up."

"Why? You're not insinuating *I'm* a suspect, are you, Detective Reardon?"

"Not yet, Kirt. But Doris did always pick the wrong guys." He smirked, stepping back into the cold snow and wind.

****

They drove with resistance, the snow heaps on the road hampering their progression.

"That kid—what was his name?" Charlie said.

"Tommy Nescott?"

"Yah. Was he the one from the alley?"

"Yup. Kid's messed up. Someone scared him good."

Static poured out of the CB radio unit in the dashboard. "Any available unit, please respond," said the dispatcher.

Sam picked up the microphone and keyed it up. "Dispatch, this is Detectives Duncan and Reardon. Over."

"What's your forty?"

"Just off Pine, near the Madson mansion."

The storm howled, making the voice of Helen Ellison, the dispatcher, hard to hear. "We need an officer down at the Clock Diner. There's been report of a homicide. But we'll patch it through to the next available unit."

"Not a problem. We're a couple blocks away. We'll take a look. Over." Sam replaced the mike on the hook.

"Copy that."

"What in the world is going on tonight?" Sam said.

Charlie wiped sweaty palms on his pants. He dreaded to think of who they might find dead at the diner. But with the note from Tommy Nescott buried deep in his pocket, he had a hunch. Susan. Doris.

Could just be a coincidence. He'd know for sure once he got to the Clock.

"You all right, Chuck?"

Charlie turned, as if forgetting Sam was in the car. "Yeah, just wondering the same as you, what's going on." He looked out the window at the falling snow. "Maybe something to do with this storm."

"How do you mean?"

"I don't know. Don't you ever wonder if there's something else out there?"

Sam laughed. "You mean like Bigfoot?"

"No, I don't mean like Bigfoot. I don't know." He continued to look out the window. "You know they think it was someone else besides the Egyptians who designed the pyramids? Something not human."

"Who thinks that?"

"*The National Geographic.* All the excavation projects they have going on in Egypt, they're finding these strange relics and hieroglyphs. Some say they're the demons thrown out of heaven. The Nephalim, I think they're called."

Sam turned onto Madison. The Clock Diner came into view. "So you think some demon is committing random homicides in Hartington?" He pulled into a parking space in front of the diner.

"Whoever said they were random," Charlie said, straightening his hat and getting out of the car.

****

Nancy Welch was a twenty-four-year-old waitress at the Clock Diner. Charlie's regular server, he also kept up a regular romance with her the same way he liked his eggs: over easy and on the side. They found her in the dry food storage the same as the others, open bloused and stabbed to death.

"Who called it in?" Charlie asked.

The diner's manager, Ed Pellicano, was a balding man in his mid-fifties. "I called it in," Ed said. "But Lucy found her. Just like you see her now."

"Where's Lucy?" Charlie said.

"She's pretty shook up, detective. Nancy and Lucy were close friends. Worked together for years." He wiped the back of his neck with a handkerchief. "I sure hope you find who did this. Such a shame." His eyes welled up and he grabbed a cigarette from his shirt pocket. Motioning toward the dining room, he said, "Lucy's in the back booth."

Charlie passed through the kitchen smelling grease and syrup. He pushed open the swing doors leading to the dining room. Lucy Marshall wore her strawberry blonde hair pinned up in a high bun. She smoked a cigarette with pouty lips stained with red lipstick.

"Miss Marshall?" Charlie said.

She brought up sapphire eyes.

"I'm Detective Reardon, NNPD," he said, showing his badge.

"I know who you are, detective" she said, slipping the cigarette between parted lips.

"May I sit down?"

She shrugged indifferently. Charlie slid into the booth across from her.

"I've seen you with Nancy, from time to time," she said. "She was a good friend."

Charlie removed his hat and set it on the table. "You wanna tell me what happened?"

She let out a deep breath. "We were closing up for the night. Nancy was cleaning in the back while I straightened tables in the dining room. I didn't hear anything out of the ordinary." Tears dampened her eyes. She brought them up to meet Charlie's. "She really liked you. She always said you were the kind of guy she could settle down with, not that I understood what she saw. Nancy was always attracted to the wrong type of guys."

It was a low blow, but he let her have it. "Could we just focus on what happened here tonight, Miss Marshall?"

"I am, detective."

Charlie sat back, the vinyl crunching like cellophane beneath him. "I'm not sure I'm following. What does my relationship with Nancy have to do with her being murdered?"

She pressed her cigarette butt into the ashtray, twisted it until the cherry burnt out, and wiped a fresh tear off her cheek. "A man came in earlier this evening. I'd never seen him before and figured he was just passing through. He came up to Nancy, and I was standing right next to her." She lit another cigarette, blew out the smoke. "He told her that no sin goes unpunished, and everything that goes around comes around."

"What was that supposed to mean?"

Lucy shrugged. "I don't know. We thought he was just crazy or drunk. He gave me the creeps."

Charlie leaned forward, his fingers tapping the table. Lucy looked around the diner, eyes like a panicked deer in headlights. "Here," she said, passing a square of paper across the table, her voice in a whisper. "He told me to give you this."

Charlie's mouth went dry as the paper slid between his fingers. A high-pitched ringing filled his ears.

"I don't know how he knew you'd be back tonight. But he did." She was shaking now, her cigarette teetering like a seesaw in her hand. "If you had something to do with this...I swear to God."

Charlie stared at Lucy, waiting for her to lift her eyes. "I cared about Nancy. I don't know who that guy was or who did this, but it's my job to find out. Even if it kills me."

Lucy's lip quivered and she nodded before facing the window.

Through the glass, Charlie watched the forensics unit pull up. He stood without a word, leaving Lucy alone to find Sam in the back with Al. Charlie pulled him off to the side. "We need to get back to the station. I want to see if they learned anything new from the autopsies."

Ed shuffled over. "Well, detectives, it looks like there isn't much more I can do here. I'd like to go home. It's been a hell of a night and that storm looks like it's turning into a blizzard."

"I understand how hard this must be for you," Sam said. "Unfortuntaely, you're gonna need to be available for questioning by forensics while they collect evidence. Shouldn't take long."

Ed pursed his mouth and nodded. "Guess I should get Lucy to put on a pot of coffee."

"That's a good idea," Charlie said. "Sorry for the inconvenience."

"I understand. I just want this day to be over."

As the detectives left the diner they exchanged a brief conversation with the passing forensics team and coroner heading in. The storm grew to a squall, and Charlie thought Ed Pellicano wasn't far off from believing it might turn into a blizzard.

****

The howling wind carried a bite, and Charlie squinted in the sideways falling snow, his arm blocking his nose and mouth, his fedora pulled far down over his eyes. He swung the precinct door open and stepped inside. Immediately the howling ceased. The heat welcomed him while he shook off the snow.

"I'm starting to think you might be right about the storm, Chuck," Sam said, standing beside him. "I've lived here my whole life and I've never seen anything like this."

Charlie walked to his desk, peeling out of his coat and hat along the way. He set them down and moved to the secretaries' desk. "Hey, June, they find out anything new on the Doris Lane murder?"

June was in her late forties with large glasses attached to a beaded string around her neck. "Not much. Here's the preliminary report." She handed Charlie a manila folder.

"Thanks. What about for—" He couldn't say it.

June's mouth turned in a slim frown, her voice softened as she said, "Not yet, Charlie. I was so sorry to hear about Susan."

Charlie nodded. "Thanks. Just let me know."

He hurried to his desk. Opening the file, he let out a small gasp. The photo on top showed a grotesque version of Doris Lane, her chest carved up, her eyes wide and lifeless. He turned the photo face down.

The first page detailed the extent of the lacerations, the medical terms and phrases, and the science of how those conclusions came about. The second page listed the volume of major organs, loss of blood, and the presence of a sulfuric acid residue near the points of impact in and around the victim's chest.

"Sulfuric Acid?" Charlie said to himself.

"Tell me what you've got," Sam said. "That the first vic's prelim?"

Charlie cringed. He didn't like hearing Doris referred to as the 'first vic.' Charlie closed the file and passed it to Sam. "See for yourself."

After a few minutes, Sam said, "Sulfuric acid? What's that from? A rusty knife?"

"I haven't a clue." But really, he did. The second note from Lucy Marshall explained it all.

"This is just a preliminary report anyway. If there's more, the coroner will find it." He looked up. Charlie was staring at him.

"I'm gonna get out of here," Charlie said, his eyes burdened.

Sam set down the file. "Sure, partner. I'll give you a lift."

"Nah," Charlie said, pressing on his hat and coat. "I'm gonna walk."

Sam laughed. "It's a blizzard, Charlie. You can't walk in that."

Charlie stared out the window barely able to see the sidewalk. "Sam I lost Susan tonight. I may have left her six years ago, but she's gone forever now." He faced Sam, his eyes pooled with tears. He wanted to tell him about Doris, how he'd spent shifts on the clock in her arms, using allocated funds to buy her time and front the hour at a cheap motel. He wanted to tell him about Nancy, how he said he loved her to sleep with her when it was convenient, but ignored her when it wasn't. He wanted to.

But he didn't.

"I just need to be alone," Charlie said, and he stepped out the door, and disappeared into the storm.

****

Charlie leaned into the force of wind, his fedora long gone. His visibility less than a foot in any direction, he pressed through, his body aching and numb. Out of nowhere, he approached a crossroads. A man stood in the cortex wearing a black trench coat, dark as night, and a hat that cast a long shadow covering his face. Charlie stopped before him, the scent of rotten eggs and vomit faint.

"You the guy sending me messages?" Charlie asked.

The stranger nodded.

"And you, you murdered those women?"

The stranger nodded again.

"Why?"

"Because, detective, a sin cannot go unpunished. I would think you of all people would understand that one. The penalty for the crime."

"So, who are you? The devil?"

"Not quite. I am more of an employee." He tilted his hat back, showing albino skin against red eyes which grew black as if replaced by two pieces of coal.

Charlie staggered back with a gasp. "What are you?"

"I am exactly who you want me to be. Or would you prefer this body?" He changed, morphing into Nancy, then Susan, then Doris. "Are you surprised Charlie?"

"You're a demon."

"Good old Charlie. A detective 'til the end." The demon smiled, exposing Doris's white teeth.

Charlie clenched his fists, fighting back tears. "So what do you want with me?"

"I think you already know."

He was right. He knew exactly what the demon wanted. Charlie pictured the grotesque, lifeless women lying in their blood, women he had shared a warm bed with, women whom he had loved in one way or another. All innocent. All punished for his lust and desires. Tears fell unguarded from his eyes.

The demon stepped closer. "The choice is yours. My price is your soul with one condition."

"What?"

"Normally my contracts are for ten years. But your situation is precarious. Your soul is worth one. However, I would be willing to make a trade. All ten years for the others."

Charlie's insides raged. "You set me up. I don't have a choice."

"We always have a choice, Charlie." The demon in Doris's skin moved closer, caressing his cheek. "Your choices have brought you to this crossroads."

He threw her hand away. "And what if I say no?"

The demon shrugged. "Everything stays the same. You go on living in your pathetic little world with all the burdens you carry." She clasped her hands at her chest, tapping her fingertips together. "But if you say yes…the possibilities are endless."

Charlie stared in the distance. He couldn't escape his fate. He felt doomed at whichever road he chose. But he could at least make things right. With a quick breath, Charlie wiped his eyes. "All right," he said. "Let's finish this."

A deal was struck. The demon resembling Doris smiled, leaning in close. "I'm so glad you chose yes."

With a kiss, the dotted line was signed, and with what felt like Doris's lips still pressed against his own, Charlie clutched his chest and slumped face down into the drifts of snow. Both the blizzard and the demon had vanished.

****

Sam Duncan sat at his desk in the center of the homicide department taking a call. "He's not in yet…sure, I can take a look at it…yup…see you in a few."

Sam put on his hat and coat and left the precinct. He bundled his jacket tighter and climbed into his police cruiser. As he passed the Clock Diner he saw Nancy Welch bussing a booth near the front window. On the sidewalk just outside the diner, stood a call girl named Doris Lane. Lightly falling snow collected in her blonde hair curling out from beneath a Russian fur hat. Sam was driving to Susan Reynolds's house. Her boiler was out again. Maybe.

THE PRIEST

1.

The saloon doors swung open with a creak as heavy winds wailed outside. The man stumbled in, and the bartender never would have thought twice about him or given him a second glance, if it hadn't been for the squirrelly look in his eyes.

"Sarah," Jedediah whispered to the young girl standing beside him behind the bar. "Go on in the back and get a message out."

"To whom?" She stared up with her mother's green eyes. Dark hair tumbled across her shoulders. Sarah regarded the sweat-covered man as he crept across the saloon floor mumbling beneath his breath. A thin comb-over raked by the wind stood upright as a scarecrow on top of his head.

"Okay, papa." Sarah turned on her heels and scurried away.

"Hello there, stranger," Jedediah's voice boomed. "Can I fetch you a drink?"

The man teetered toward the bar, much in the way most men left it. His darting eyes finally found their way to Jedediah's face.

"There you go," Jedediah said, coaxing a baby. "Come on, now. Take a seat."

Slowly, the muttering man slid – he was barefoot, Jedediah now noticed – across the sawdust laden floor and into an empty barstool. Jedediah set a glass of whiskey before him. "Looks like you need one."

The man wasted no time slamming the drink back. Jedediah minded the dirt beneath his very long fingernails. "What's your name, fellow?"

The man set down the glass and Jedediah refilled it on instinct. "It's Frances Deveaux." He sipped the whiskey with shaking hands. The wind wailed louder.

"What brings you to these parts, Mr. Deveaux?" Jedediah asked, on account of the man's northern accent.

"Business."

The doors flew into the hardwood walls by a heavy gust and Mr. Deveaux nearly jumped out of his skin.

Jedediah motioned for Bobbie Ray, a dark-haired kid who worked for him from time to time, to close the doors. "A bit on edge tonight?"

Frances Deveaux turned around to face the bar top. His hands had stopped shaking. The fog shrouding his mind seemed to have lifted. He trained his now clear eyes upon Jedediah's. "Guess I am."

He had a good face, as far as Jedediah was concerned, rounded with a long nose and thick brows. A five o'clock shadow covered his cheeks and chin.

"What's got you so scared?" Jedediah fidgeted with an already clean tumbler, taking a towel to it inside and out. Sweat beaded on his closely shaven head. His handlebar moustache tickled his upper lip.

Frances Deveaux's hands started rattling again, as if whatever had possessed him earlier had returned. "She...tried to...kill me!" His bulging blue eyes locked on Jedediah's steel grays. "I had to do it..."

A train horn blared through the air from the nearby station. Wind banged the shutters. The doors flapped with a heavy bang. Frances Deveaux shook his head, maybe trying to remember, most likely trying to forget.

Bobbie Ray inched to within an arm's reach of the man, his Winchester hidden beneath his long coat.

Jedediah reached for the Colt Peacemaker he carried in his holster. "Why's there dirt beneath your nails, sir? What'd you do to her?"

Frances Deveaux's smile lurched across his face, demented as the Devil himself. His teeth hung in pointy rows like a weatherworn picket fence. "I gave her what she wanted."

"What was that, Mr. Deveaux?"

His eyes floated lifeless in his head and his neck bent unnaturally to the side. A new voice rolled off his tongue, and said, "Yooouuuu!"

The thing inside of Frances Deveaux lunged across the bar, swiping long fingernails at Jedediah the way a honey badger swipes its claws. Jedediah leapt. Frances Deveaux's body slammed into the bottle display that crashed to the ground alongside him. Glass splinters stuck to his face glinted in the light of the kerosene lamps.

He growled spraying blood stained spittle through the air. Jedediah got off a shot. The bullet sunk into Frances Deveaux's shoulder, knocked his frame off-kilter, but the man didn't flinch. He just kept coming.

"Good, God," Jedediah muttered, as Frances Deveaux inched closer. "Sarah!" Jedediah pumped a few rounds into the undead's chest. "You send that message yet?"

"He's coming, Papa!"

"Don't you come out here." Jedediah pulled the trigger to an empty chamber. With no time to reload, he grabbed a chair and flung it. The wood crunched with Frances Deveaux's nose and broke them both. Jedediah side-glanced the bar. It had emptied.

Except for Bobbie Ray.

He was a skinny kid with brown eyes set close together. But he was fearless. He stood in a wide fighting stance with one hand gripping his knife, the other his gun. He smirked. "Looks like you're needing some help."

"What the hell you gonna do with that knife?" Jedediah spat. "You don't even know how to use it." He dodged out of the way of Frances Deveaux's body, which smacked into a table before hitting the floor.

Bobbie Ray staggered closer to the brawl, swinging his knife at the creature in long strides. Frances Deveaux snarled, swatting the knife out of Bobbie Ray's hand as if it was a playing card. The knife landed with a clink on the floor. Panicked, Bobbie Ray aimed his gun, shooting off six rounds into everything but Frances Deveaux.

"Damn it all, Bobbie Ray. What the hell are you doing?"

"Helping." He eyed the walls where his rounds had wedged.

The wind howled. The shutters slammed. Frances

Deveaux screeched inhuman sounds. Jedediah had no more ammo, and wasn't about to risk Sarah's life by having her bring him more. He turned to Bobbie Ray. "Lay a line of salt in front of the door. This may not be the only one."

Bobbie Ray pulled a satchel from his hip and marked the beginnings of a crooked salt line across the threshold. The saloon doors blew open whacking Bobbie Ray in the head and sending him to the floor unconscious.

Jedediah turned, hopeful.

It was just the wind. In the split second when his attention faltered, Frances Deveaux barreled into Jedediah. The air left his lungs as his back cracked against the floor. His whole body screamed in silent pain. The sound on life itself had been shut off. But the serrated teeth grinding into his shoulder kept him grounded in reality. His eyes rolled back. Jedediah prayed.

He could see in flickers, the way lightning bolts light up the trees and things in the darkness when the heart of the storm passes overhead. In an instant, Frances Deveaux was ripped off Jedediah and flung across the room. He gulped air into his burning lungs. Jedediah's hearing returned as a ping that evolved into muted voices.

The man who had set Jedediah free wore a charcoal gray trench coat and cowboy hat. He carried a flaming scythe in one hand, a glowing rifle strapped tight across his back. In an ancient tongue, brandishing the scythe high above his head, he swung through the air in a wide arc. The flame sliced through the body of Frances Deveaux with a supernatural crack. Frances

Deveaux fell dead to the floor. The blade didn't cut into his flesh.

It fractured his soul.

Sarah ran over to Jedediah. Bobbie Ray had come to and was staggering over to help.

"Get him to his feet," Sarah ordered.

"Watch my shoulder," Jedediah said. "Hurts like a son of a bitch."

Sarah slipped beneath his wounded arm while Bobbie Ray slipped under the other one. They led Jedediah to a seat that hadn't been overturned during the fight.

The cowboy knelt before him, pulling back Jedediah's shirt to scrutinize the wound. His face remained hidden by the wide brim of his hat. He wore hide boots whose origin Jedediah could only speculate and his skin smelled like fire.

"It's not too deep," the cowboy said. "Won't take me a minute." He pressed his large flat palm against the wound.

Jedediah bit the inside of his cheek to keep from screaming. His mouth pooled with the iron-taste of his own blood.

The cowboy lifted his hand.

Jedediah stared as the gaping holes in his flesh were completely healed; the tear in his blood soaked shirt was all that remained. "Well, I'll be damned."

"Be careful, bartender. You don't meant it." He leaned over the body of what had once been Frances Deveaux and whatever had tried to eat Jedediah. "This one's dead."

"Course he is," Bobbie Ray said. "You killed him."

"No. This man's *been* dead." The cowboy rolled the body on to its stomach with the steel-tipped toe of his boot. "Was before he walked through those doors."

"The living dead?" Bobbie Ray whispered.

"Of all the unholy things," said Sarah.

Beneath Frances Deveaux's shoulder blade lay an empty cavity where his liver should have been.

"Detestable." Sarah covered her mouth and swept to an empty seat near the bar.

"Did he say why he was here?" the cowboy asked, staring at the body.

"Not precisely. Just said some woman tried to kill him, so he gave her what she wanted."

"And what was that?"

Jedediah gulped hard. "Me."

The man looked up, his face in shadows. "You?"

"That's right."

"Did she say what for?"

"Never got to that part."

The man didn't say a word as he stared at Jedediah. Finally, he spoke. "Something's after you, Jed. I'm gonna stay in town a while to figure out what." He looked up. "You okay with that?"

His eyes shone in a radiant shade of violet. Dirty-blond hair fell ragged from beneath his hat.

"Yes, Simeon. I'm okay with it," Jedediah said. "I think I'm gonna need some help on this one."

"First thing to figure out is where this man's liver went. Hopefully, it will lead to this woman you mentioned." Simeon stood, walked back to the entrance, and turned in the doorway. "You all better get your feet shod," he said with a smirk, tipping his hat, "because it's about to get ugly."

2.

The wind whipped all around him as Simeon headed down the dusty main street. He had traveled this road before. The long stretch lay between lines of wooden buildings: a hardware store, Martha's Sundries, a blacksmith's shop, the coffin-makers warehouse. Few souls walked the streets at this late hour. Even the moon stayed in tonight, hidden behind thick clouds, unwilling to bear witness to whatever evil lurked in the darkness.

The heavy clomp of horse hooves neared in the dusty wind. Two black stallions with eyes of fire appeared through the mist, drawing a black, driverless carriage as cold as Death. Simeon watched the carriage as it passed, catching the eyes of its fare; bright golden-yellow eyes on a porcelain face with delicate features. Silver-blonde hair that begged to be caressed. Her smile was pure ecstasy and lust coursed through Simeon's veins. She spoke in a whisper without moving her sensuous lips and Simeon trained his eyes upon them.

"Be gone," he said.

And with a blink, the carriage, the horses, and the stunning fare disappeared.

Simeon stood for a moment, gaping at the empty street aborted by the carriage. The wind screeched, as if mocking him for entertaining the vision for so long. Tendrils of his hair whipped him in the face. His heavy heart needed encouragement. He plodded on, his boots now laden with dust, and entered the sanctuary of a nearby church.

The silence eddied as he crossed the entryway. The door closed out the grasping wind, which beckoned him to return. He passed the Holy Water, stepped down the aisle – his spurs clinking with each stride – to the first row pew. His face fell into his cupped hands and he wept.

"Forgive me, Father," he whispered.

"God's love covers all sins, my son," a voice spoke.

Simeon lifted his head, wiping his face dry. He stared up at the small-framed man, young, barely into his twenties, with short, sand-colored hair and blue eyes.

"Not all sins, Father," Simeon said, bitterly.

The clergyman took a seat on the empty pew beside him. "Tell me what you have done and I will give you penance for your absolution."

He had a good soul, Simeon could tell, and even in his youth he'd experienced much of the evil roaming the Earth. "I lusted after a woman."

The man smiled kindly. "The lust of the flesh can be powerful and destructive. Did you act upon these thoughts?"

"No."

"Good. It seems you have heeded the words of Solomon by taking Wisdom and Understanding as your kin. *'For they will keep you from the strange woman, which flattereth with her tongue.'* Proverbs seven, verse four."

The tiny hairs on Simeon's neck stood out on end. "The harlot. The seductress."

A broad grin spread across the clergyman's face. "You are well-versed. Then you already know the blood of the Son cleanses all who believe."

"I believe in God," Simeon said. "The question is does he believe in me?"

The clergyman's face blanched, taken aback by Simeon's statement. "Who are you, stranger?"

"They call me The Priest. But I am merely a fallen one seeking redemption."

Their eyes locked.

"Close your eyes, father," Simeon said. "Let me show you."

The clergyman complied, and Simeon placed his large hand over his eyes. Instantly, the man's mind flooded with images. He gasped, yanked free of Simeon's touch, his skin covered in sweat. "You are a demon?" He backed away in repulsion.

"A fallen angel," Simeon corrected. "My name was once Vengeance."

"Why have you come to defile the house of God?" the clergyman seethed.

"I haven't, Father. I am merely seeking sanctuary."

"You will find none here."

Simeon plodded back to the door. He turned to face the man. "'*Vengeance is mine,*' sayeth the Lord. Ain't that right, Father?"

The man did not answer.

"I have to believe it's true. That even someone like me can find forgiveness." Simeon treaded into the street, leaving the clergyman behind. He didn't blame him for how he felt. Simeon knew what he was. He just hoped he could perform enough good deeds to earn his way back into God's good graces, before his kind was thrown into the Lake of Fire forever.

3.

Bobbie Ray Wilcox left the saloon, his hands buried deep in his pockets. Whirling winds pushed against him. He had seen evil tonight, incarnate, but it wasn't the first time. After inhabiting with Jedediah for all these years, he'd encountered dozens of sinful men and women possessed by demons.

Tonight had been the worst.

He'd studied the written word, the sea scrolls detailing the engagement of fallen ones; Nephalim in Mesopotamia who had bred with human women to produce demi-gods worshiped by ancient man. He owned a stockpile of weapons for killing demons that had been willed by his father, Rankin Wilcox, which had been past down the Wilcox Family Tree for countless generations.

They were demon hunters.

Bobbie Ray hadn't known all this until he'd met Jedediah. He'd explained things to him in plain terms, which terrified Bobbie Ray at the time. Now, he was guileless of those beings that shared his world, seeking hosts to contain their evil spirits while they wreaked havoc on the planet. They'd take out as many of God's creation as they could before their time was up.

Not on his watch.

The stairs leading up to his lodging above the meat market came sooner than he'd expected. A woman stood on the corner near the street, and Bobbie Ray jumped in surprise. "Evening, ma'am," he said, politely.

"Evening yourself," she said with a soft smile.

Warmth flushed through Bobbie Ray's body. He

found himself backpedaling the few steps he'd taken.

"You live here?" she asked.

Bobbie Ray simply nodded.

Her silver-blonde hair blew in the breeze, not tattered and whipped like his, but softly off her shoulders, revealing her slender neck. She wore black lace with tall boots disappearing beneath a chiffon skirt. Her tiny waist beckoned to be touched. Her strapless corset lifted ample breasts. She smiled and dimples settled in her cheeks.

Bobbie Ray locked on her almond-shaped eyes, and said, "Yes."

She stared, quizzically. "Yes, what?"

"Yes, ma'am. I live here. " He snapped out of his stupor. "I'm sorry, you just startled me."

"Oh, I'm begging your pardon." She turned to leave.

He hurried to stop her. "I meant I'm surprised to see someone as beautiful as you unaccompanied so late in the evening."

She faced him. "My horse threw a shoe at the edge of town and I've been looking for someone to give me a hand. My husband's out on business and—"

"You're married?" Bobbie Ray said his countenance fading.

"Yes, sir. I am. It seems the whole town's indoors, on account of the winds, and ain't no one been around to help. Till you."

She shimmied closer, and Bobbie Ray watched her hips sway, her breasts gently bounce, her hair slightly blow. "I could sure use your help, if you're willing."

Bobbie Ray felt his blood spread out from his stomach in waves. "I'm willing."

The woman drew closer still, her breasts nearly touching his chest. "I hoped you would be," she said, as she pressed her lips against his.

4.

Jedediah lay fast asleep. His dream was a replay of the creature that had attacked him in the saloon, coming closer and closer. Only this time, Simeon didn't answer his message. The searing from the bite in his shoulder returned and he woke from the pain. Simeon stood beside his bed staring down at him.

"Jesus," Jedediah said, clutching his chest. "You scared the hell out of me."

"Didn't want to wake you, Jed."

"Wake me the next time." Jedediah sat on the edge of his bed in his red long johns. "It's creepy to open my eyes and see you standing there just staring at me."

Simeon crossed to the rocking chair in the corner of the room, made of the same cherry wood as the four-poster bed and dresser drawers. He took off his hat and set it on a round table covered with a white eyelet cloth. "It's a harlot," Simeon said, "the one Solomon warned of."

Jedediah brushed back the edges of his handlebar moustache. "The one that wants me?"

"Yup."

"What do you think she wants with me?"

Simeon shrugged. "She's got a nice little set-up here. A small town filled with mostly folks passing through to the bigger cities. Hell, that's why you stay here. Makes it harder to stick out and get noticed when people don't stick around."

Jedediah stared at the hardwood floor, lost in thought. "What makes you think it's the same woman Solomon spoke of?"

"The Proverb talks about the man seduced by this woman being like a snared bird, not knowing it's his life he's trading for pleasure." Simeon paused, drawing out the point. "Also says he'd figure it out when a dart strikes through his liver."

Jedediah turned, one eyebrow raised in skepticism. "It says that?"

"Sure does. And that many strong men have been slain by her."

"Sounds like our woman." Jedediah turned sharply. "Wonder what she wants with me."

"Someone like you could make things problematic for someone like her."

Jedediah seethed through closed teeth, sucking in air. His hand reached for his wounded shoulder.

"Takes a while to fully heal." Simeon stood and placed his hat atop his head. "I'm gonna go and—" His words cut out. His head jerked skyward. His eyes rolled back.

"Simeon?" Jedediah asked his voice shaky.

A faint glow emanated from the fallen angel as his arms rose, palms facing up. Slowly, he lifted off the ground. The room began to quake and tremble. Hanging pictures crashed to the floor. Bottles rolled off the dresser and shattered. The glowing light became blinding.

Jedediah's door flew open. A panicked look covered Sarah's face as she stood dumbfounded in the doorway. Simeon glowed brighter and brighter, till Jedediah had to shield his eyes. With a tremor that blew out the windows, Simeon's spirit produced a wail.

Sarah fell to the floor screaming, crying, petrified.

Jedediah covered his head, howling through grinding teeth. Until it all suddenly stopped.

And Simeon was gone.

5.

Bobbie Ray opened the front door of his lodging and slipped inside. He grabbed a kerosene lamp and quickly lit it. The room was an open space with a water basin against the far wall. A fireplace with two wooden chairs angled to face it sat on the opposite wall beside a mattress covered with carelessly tossed blankets.

"Come on in," he told the woman. "I'll light a fire."

She stepped tentatively inside. Her eyes scanned the room and settled on the stacks of books and scrolls beside the mattress. "You're a scholar?" she asked, crossing the room and reaching for a book.

"Don't touch that." Bobbie Ray snatched the book from her delicate hand.

Her golden eyes sharpened into slits, like a cat's.

"They belonged to my father." Bobbie Ray placed the book back on the stack and returned to the hearth. He layered the wood and tinder, then lit the fire.

"What's your name?" The woman sat on his mattress. The springs creaked as she hiked her skirt and slowly unlaced her boots.

He inched closer. "Name's Bobbie Ray Wilcox."

"I'm Haven." She slipped off her other boots, her

skirt lifted high up on her tone thigh. "You don't mind, do you?"

"No, ma'am. Not at all." His eyes grazed down her neck to the shadow of her cleavage outlining her breasts.

"No one would know," she whispered, unlatching her corset in the back, hook by hook.

Bobbie Ray swallowed hard, dumbstruck by her proposition. "What about your husband?" He ran his fingers through his dark hair and watched her corset fall to the floor revealing her creamy white skin.

She stood, and her skirt fell beside her corset. He eyed every inch of her. He wanted to feel her velvety skin, to be inside her. He would give anything for it.

"I won't tell," she said, sprawling out on his mattress.

Bobbie Ray didn't move for a moment. Then, he began throwing off his clothes, his shirt busting buttons. He hopped on his free foot while he yanked off his boot, until he was naked. He fell into her arms where they kissed and stroked. His insides shook as her body entwined with his.

This is wrong, he heard a still small voice whisper.

But he didn't care. He wanted Haven more than he'd ever wanted anything in his entire life. "I think I've died and gone to Heaven," he moaned, his body rocking on top of hers.

Her lips stretched into a long smile that struck Bobbie Ray as odd. There was something he knew or should have known if he could have thought clearly.

"You got the first part right," Haven said, and she plunged her long nails deep into his back.

6.

Simeon jolted up, his indigo eyes darting all around him. He stood, his chiseled back tense, wavy hair grazing his shoulders. He was no longer in Jedediah's room, no longer in the ghost town where he lived. Not even in the same dimension anymore.

He'd been called away.

The acrid air warned him of the presence. He braced with thick legs and outstretched arms in anticipation for a force he could not yet see. From his peripheral view, the foul smell rapidly took form as a large, black beast charged and tackled his six-foot frame. The creature's impact knocked Simeon to the ground. They wrestled and scraped for an upper hand, exchanging blows as they rolled across the sandy terrain.

The creature clawed black, triangular fingertips into Simeon's triceps and he screamed out in agony. Favoring his injured arm, Simeon grappled with the beast by wrapping his good arm around its wheezing neck in a tight grip. The beast broke free, released its claws, and pounced to a high branch of a nearby tree where it crouched like a panther, watching Simeon with yellow eyes, panting hot rattling breaths, and waiting for the optimal moment to finish the attack.

Simeon removed a small three-inch diamond-tipped scroll etched with the scriptures of truth resembling a shotgun shell, and pulled the leather strap holding his 12-gauge off his back. His eyes never left the creature, which now sat near the tree's crown. Simeon scowled at the beast while he opened the breach and slipped in the shell, closing the action to lock the scroll into place. The muscles in his arm tensed as Simeon lifted the butt of the gun with one arm and set it on his shoulder, his cheek grazing the cold metal. He took aim, clicked off the safety, and abruptly pulled the trigger.

The beast wheezed in terror as the scroll struck in the small of its back, lurching when the diamond tip sliced deep into its black flesh where the truth exploded. The demon writhed and shrieked vehement curses as supernatural light from the scroll's etchings seeped into the bloody wound and glowed through the creature's orifices.

With a fire in his eyes, Simeon raised his free-hand and proclaimed, "I command you to roam the Dry Wasteland in spirit form!"

With a pop and a tear, the sky behind Fear ripped violently open, sucking the shrieking demon to another realm. The instant it disappeared, the blue sky and white clouds returned, sealing the hole as if nothing had ever happened.

Simeon studied the wound on his triceps where Fear had clutched him. The black holes left behind burned and his muscles throbbed. The wound would need attending to. In the distance, Simeon spotted a massive mist approaching.

Joel.

Joel hovered before him, his eyes like vapors of water rising in a mist. His straight, black hair flowed in perpetual motion, as if submersed in a tumultuous river. They stared at each other for some time.

"I see Fear caught a hold of you," Joel said in disapproval.

"Not before I sent that scum to the Wasteland."

Simeon's eyes were drawn close.

Joel studied Simeon, his head leaning to the side. "What is it you needed?" he asked.

"I need to know about the harlot spoken of in Proverbs seven."

"You mean the death Angel," Joel said, gliding over to a rock beneath the tree.

"Tell me about her."

"What do you want to know?"

"How to kill her."

Joel laughed. "Not such an easy task to accomplish. You're talking about the spirit of Jezebel, not some simple whore."

Simeon felt his brow furrow. "Jezebel?"

"Yes. A powerful seductress who is able to control men who are more inclined to be led by their lustful desires."

"Control them to do what?"

"Whatever it is she wants."

Joel sat on the rock, his hair no longer floating, though his eyes still toggled, staring at Simeon pacing the grass. "What is this about, Simeon?"

Simeon looked up. "She's after someone I know, and she's killing men in his town."

"Jedediah? The witness?"

"Yes."

With a contemptuous look, Joel said, "That changes everything. The scrolls will soon be opened, but the two witnesses must still be protected. You will need this," he said. His fingers swirled in a circle, revealing his palm, which held an emerald studded dagger. "This belonged to King Solomon. It will take care of your demon."

Simeon took the dagger, spinning it between his fingers to scatter the light.

"And Simeon," Joel said.

The fallen angel looked up.

"At all costs you must protect Jedediah. His life is the only one that holds worth."

Simeon nodded.

"And if you do well, God may still offer you salvation. Though it is undeserved."

Simeon gritted his teeth. "God's forgiveness is for everyone."

"Not for the fallen," Joel said, his voice rising. "You made your choice when you denied your Creator."

"We were lied to!" Simeon shouted. "All of us!"

Joel shrugged. "So you say. Only God knows the truth."

"Then let Him be the judge." Simeon seethed, disgusted by Joel's arrogance, his shoulders rising with each heaving breath.

Joel stood, his hair and garments once again floating in an invisible breeze. "Just keep the witness safe." The vapors in Joel's eyes swelled, the mist enveloped his body, and he dissipated into a cloud of nothingness.

Simeon took in a deep breath. Hot air blew across his tacky skin as he scanned the desert horizon. He slid the dagger into the hilt around his waist and closed his eyes. "God, help me."

And in that instant, he too, was gone.

7.

Bobbie Ray writhed as the demon's claws sunk in. Blood squirted from the punctures running hot down his bare back. Haven's face had taken on its ancient form. Her skin scorched in red and black embers. Her eyes glowed. Her spiked teeth plunged deep into his neck.

Bobbie Ray screamed. His fingertips fumbled for the book just within his grasp. He couldn't breathe as she sandwiched him in a vice-like grip between teeth and claw. He stretched farther. His fingers gripped the spine and he slammed the heavy book into the side of Haven's head, sending her tumbling off the mattress.

Bobbie Ray rushed to the loose floorboard near the fireplace. His secret stash of stockpiled weapons. Haven was crouched on her feet, growling at him. His dripping blood covered her chin. He lifted the edge of the floorboard as Haven hurtled through the air. Bobbie Ray rolled. She slammed into the mantel and fell into the fire.

"You crazy bitch!"

Haven righted herself. Her body smoked where the embers smoldered on her skin. Her eyes locked on Bobbie Ray.

The oak chair lay near his feet. He lifted it, straining against the heavy wood, and winged it at Haven as she charged him. The chair cracked against her torso and knocked her back into the flames.

Sweat dripped down Bobbie Ray's face stinging his eyes. *What the hell am I gonna do?* Panicked, he frantically searched the room. His gaze locked on the gun and knife wedged in his holster on top of his clothes. He looked at Haven. She was up again, standing, though her frame was lopsided; her hips having done a three-quarter turn and pulled her whole frame grotesquely askew.

He lunged forward toppling his clothes as Haven attempted to attack. Bobbie Ray reached his holster and tried to work his gun free. The chamber snagged on the leather. With a sideways glance, he could see Haven stumbling closer.

"Damn it!" Bobbie Ray hissed. "Get the hell out!"

After some trying, he wriggled the gun free, and rolled onto his back, barrel pointed up. Haven stood over top of him.

He pulled the trigger.

Nothing.

"Are you shitting me?"

He threw the empty gun at Haven's face, cracking her nose, before the gun bounced off and hit the floor.

"What's wrong, Bobbie Ray?" Haven asked. "Don't want me no more?"

"Stay away from me, you fucking...demon whore!"

"It's Death Angel," she said, inching closer. "I figured you'd have known with all those books and scrolls you've studied."

Bobbie Ray blinked hard. "Stupid! Idiot!" he snarled at himself.

"Not so much," Haven said. "I need to get close to Jedediah and your body will be the perfect host."

"Why?"

"Because he's one of the two witnesses John spoke about in the book of Revelation. If I can get inside you, I can kill him and prevent the prophecy from coming to pass. I can keep the Son of God from the second coming."

"You're crazy!"

"It's the least you can do," Haven mocked. "Seeing how you've completely busted up this body."

Bobbie Ray slipped his hand into his holster, slowly pulling his knife free. "He'll know," Bobbie Ray said, trying to distract her.

Haven laughed. "No, he won't. I just have to act stupid and follow him around everywhere asking dumb questions. He'll never notice the difference."

"You're a real bitch," Bobbie Ray said, gripping his knife.

"I get that a lot. Men tend to desire me less once they figure out who I really am."

"A hideously ugly demon?"

Haven glowered at Bobbie Ray, her sharp teeth grinding. "I was a queen once. Jezebel. A beautiful, powerful woman."

"Who dogs ate."

Haven's claws stretched into six inch sickles. "They'll feed you to the Hellhounds when I'm finished."

Haven screamed a horrible, deafening shriek and dove for Bobbie Ray. He bellowed, lifting his knife to defend himself, but it never touched her. The room filled with light, bleaching everything white.

Simeon stood behind Haven.

He wedged an emerald studded dagger deep into her back, piercing her liver. Haven stopped midstride. Her breath ceased, and she choked. Her hands gripped the tip of the blade protruding from her chest.

"I send you back to Hell," Simeon commanded as he twisted the blade and yanked it free.

Emerald light splayed through Haven's orifices.

Her body convulsed. The light intensified and her head, mouth gaping open, shot back. Light spewed out in a solid stream as her spirit emptied, returning to Hell, leaving behind nothing but a pile of ash on Bobbie Ray's floor.

8.

Two whiskey glasses clanked as Jedediah and Simeon shared a toast. Bobbie Ray held the bottle, his broken body shrouded in gauze.

Sarah carried a pan full of splintered wood. "Nice having you back, Simeon."

He set his glass down beside his hat. "Seems you called just in time."

"Be'd best if you'd come a bit sooner, next time," Bobbie Ray said. He grimaced as he scooted in his seat.

Jedediah laughed. "Serves you right, you damn fool." He took the bottle from Bobbie Ray and refilled both glasses.

Simeon studied his whiskey.

"Why do you do it?" Jedediah asked. "Heaven don't want you back. All you're doing is pissing off your kin by defecting."

Simeon set the cowboy hat on his head. "My allegiance is with my maker, even if he don't want me."

"Course he wants you," Sarah interjected. "The good Lord says, all can be redeemed."

"That's what I'm counting on. God's mercy for a traitor like me."

But it didn't matter. He'd kill demons till Hell's

lake swallowed him.
  Or God forgave him.
  Whichever came first.

MOONSHINE ON THE MISSISSIP'

PART ONE: ELI COOKE

On a perfect spring afternoon with clear blue skies and bright yellow sun, Captain Eli Cooke made a terrible mistake. A dastardly mistake. One that could've cost him his life. I told him not to do it, to think before he leapt, but…here now. I'm getting ahead of myself. Let me take you back to the beginning, to the night of the Governor's Ball.

The year was 1791. George Washington presided over the great United States of America. And the topic on the forefront on everyone's mind was alcohol, especially with the newly passed Whiskey Act to tax all illegal distilleries – moonshiners included – imposed by Secretary of State, Alexander Hamilton. A bit of a hero in my book. The March air blew cold across the Virginia plantation of Governor Henry Lee III, or 'Light-Horse Harry' as he was nicknamed during his service in the Continental Army. But the air in the dining room grew heated, damn near stifling, as a debate raged like an inferno amongst the men.

"Shiners ain't never paid no mind to the law," said Robert Memphis, a wealthy landowner from Kentucky.

"Well, they will if they know what's good for them," Light-Horse Harry chided.

"Says who?" Memphis rebutted. "The government? Why, they're sticking taxes on products they have no mind to, just to fatten their pockets."

"Looks that way," said Brett Bufone, a paunchy man from old money. "Bloody bureaucracy. Like being under Mother England's thumb all over again."

"But what about the taxes they'll bring in?" I added.

"What about them?" Memphis asked, uncaring.

"Those taxes will be used to pay for the debt accumulated during the war. A mighty large debt, might I add, which needn't come out of the people's bread money, but out of their indulgence pocketbook. A sin tax."

The Governor smiled at me as the room silenced. "Very good point, indeed, young William." His white hair, thin at the top, was pulled in a tight knot near the back of his head. "I could use a man like you in my circle."

"Thank you, sir," I said, awestruck. *Me? Working for the Governor? That would be the honor of all honors.*

"While it's all nice on paper, Mr. Lighthouse, these farmers, these shiners, will be losing more money in taxes than they'll be making in a profit. How are they supposed to feed their families?"

I considered Memphis's comment. He leaned closer, his plump forearms resting on the table, his large index finger pointing toward me. "Just 'cause they make spirits don't mean they don't have families to provide for. Do you have family, Mr. Lighthouse?"

"No, sir. I do not."

"Hmm," Memphis said, pushing off the table. "Then you couldn't possibly understand any of this."

"Having a family has nothing to do with proper taxation, Mr. Memphis," Light-Horse Harry defended. "The stability of the Union affects the married and unmarried equally. It has no prejudice for wealth or status."

"Kentucky farmers won't pay," said Memphis. "Shouldn't have to neither, what with the larger distilleries paying less tax per barrel just because they can produce more. It's not fair. Those small farms will be forced to close before winter. Then what do we have? Big business. That's all that'll be left." He stroked the tips of his black pencil mustache and stared with burning eyes at the governor.

"I agree," Bufone said. "It's as if the government under Madison's leadership wants small farmers to fail. They're cutting tax breaks to the big businesses and leaving the rest to pay fines they can't afford, forcing them to sell their farms in order to stay alive. I tell you…Mother England all over again," he repeated.

"Seeds for rebellion, is what that is," Memphis seethed.

The Governor's lilt chimed as a clock struck midnight. "If those farmers in the west mean a rebellion, Washington won't let them get away with it."

"They already have the worst of it," Bufone replied. "With the failed attempts of our arms to

protect the western frontier." He took several short sips
of his brandy, shaking his head. "Them Injuns don't
fight like gentlemen, and they've got the upper hand in
the war."

"Not to mention the damn Spaniards blocking off
the Ol' Mississip for trading," added Memphis. "Why
the hell they still hold claim to these lands is beyond
me."

The air was thick with cigar smoke as the colored
attendants set plates of cobbler in front of each man.
Like dark shadows, they just served their purpose for
the wealthy landowners.

"Where's the captain?" Light-Horse Harry asked,
turning squinted blue eyes upon me.

"He wasn't feeling well after supper," I lied,
knowing he must be feeling very well, shacked up with
the governor's fiancée, Anne Hill Carter, in an upstairs
bedroom.

"Too bad," the governor said, not sounding like he
believed my fabrication at all. "Well, gentlemen, best
finish our desserts and get back to the ball. I think
we've spoken enough about politics for one evening."

The men obliged, shoveling in cobbler and brandy
before quickly returning to the festive ballroom.

The quintet played softly in the background the
way crickets chirp unnoticed on a summer's night.
Men of social status and wealth decorated with
mistresses on their arms spoke in boisterous voices
about God only knows what. The governor's mansion
held well over five hundred souls. A marble floor
mirrored real life in cold stone. Chandeliers burned
fires above the powdered wigs and pressed suits

careening slightly in the breeze from the open clerestory windows. I stood off to the side near the punch bowl sipping gingerly and people-watching, something I was akin to do in large crowds.

"Hello, William."

I turned. Anne stood beside me, her bosom pressing out of her tight powder-blue corset.

"Evening, ma'am," I mustered, sipping more voraciously on my punch.

"Where's Eli?" she asked. Her black hair curled around her face; the rest sat high in a bun. She had dark, plain features, her nose and lips too small for her long face, but when she smiled, I couldn't help but smile back.

"I thought he was with you," I said, not thinking. My face burned. Hers blanched. "Forgive me, Miss Carter. I don't know what I'm saying." My eyes drifted to my dusty boots.

"It's quite all right, William," she said, a smile to her voice. "I'm sure I'll find him." She whisked away through the crowd, nodding at senators and congressmen, stopping to chatter with wives and mistresses – some to the same man, though only the mistress knew of the other – with all the grace and charm of a descendant of a Scottish king.

After several drinks, and no sign of the captain, I needed to visit the latrine. I crept to the outhouse around back. The flat grounds of the yard ended in hilltops covered in dogwood trees appearing as shapeless shadows in the night. Cicadas sang erratic choruses answered by bullfrogs in the pond. A cold white moon cast through the crescent and star shaped cut-outs in the wood ceiling of the outhouse.

"William!"

I jumped, splashing piss on my own leg. I peered through the slats. "Damn it, Captain! Why you gotta go sneaking up on a man when he's doing his private business?"

"Come on out of there," he said through laughter. "Pinch it off, William, and hurry up."

I finished and opened the creaking outhouse door. Captain Cooke stared at me with a smile as broad as the Union. He was a handsome man with dark hair that fell to his eyes and shoulders. A trim beard shadowed his square jaw and laugh lines, like the night did the dogwood trees, and his amber eyes read me like a gambler counting cards.

"What happened to your leg?" his course voice scratched.

I glared at him with my dirtiest look.

"How were cigars and brandy with the governor and his mindless circle of influence?"

"It wasn't mindless," I defended.

"Maybe not to the likes of you."

I glared at the captain. "You know, one of these days I'm gonna break away from you and your illegal deeds, and make a name for myself. Then how are you gonna feel?"

Eli didn't even look at me. "No, you won't, William."

My shoulders hunched. "The governor was asking for you."

Eli looked up, reading me again.

"I told him you weren't feeling well." I hated lying to the governor, especially when it was for Eli to have relations with his fiancée. But who was I to tell Eli

Cooke his business?

Eli smiled, his teeth bleached beach wood, as he slapped me on the back in approval.

"Miss Carter was looking for you," I said disdainfully.

"Oh?"

"I thought you were with her?"

"Mhm." Eli nodded. "Sure was. And the colored girl attending to her."

If there's one thing Captain Eli Cooke didn't have a shortage of it was women admirers; fat, thin, old, young, married, single, free, or slaved, he loved them all. At least in the moment.

I shook my head. "I don't see how you do it, Captain."

He pressed his open palm against his breastbone. "I'm doing my duty. Some men are born leaders, but they leave behind housefuls of women. And it's gotta be someone's job to make sure those women's needs are taken care of while their menfolk are off...leading."

My head tilted down, my eyebrows arched up. "Miss Carter's got her needs well taken care of by the man of the house."

"Not according to the sounds she was making."

I slipped my hands into my pockets, a smirk escaping my better judgment and creeping over my lips.

Eli slapped me on the back again. "Come on, now. There's someone I want you to meet."

PART TWO: AVALON STANDSLONG

Avalon Standslong was the son of a Caddo Indian Chief. He stood tall as a Redwood with glossy black hair braided clear down his lean back. He was dressed like a gentleman in a black top coat and hat, his red skin contrasting like Virginia creeper on a black wood tree. He spoke English well, having been taught by a Colonial schoolteacher who settled near the Caddo village to teach Christianity, civility, and the basics of schooling. Avalon wasn't concerned with the government's politics. Neither did he care about the war his people waged with the white man. He liked the white man. Liked their women, their curved hips and light-hued eyes and hair. And Avalon Standslong loved the white man's moonshine.

Eli led me over to the Injun standing on the veranda. His bulk grew as we moved closer, my eyes trailing up as my head tilted back. Although I knew he was civilized, according to the captain anyway, I couldn't help but think about my scalp, hoping Avalon wasn't.

"William Lighthouse, may I present Avalon Standslong," Eli said.

Avalon nodded once.

"How," I said, my flat palm facing his direction near my shoulder.

Avalon's eyes squinted sharply. Eli smacked my hand down. "What the hell's the matter with you? You ignorant bastard!"

My face must have turned as red as that Injuns. "Sorry," I muttered.

"You'll have to excuse him," Eli said, and

gesturing toward my wet pants he added, "He's barely housebroke and don't get out much."

I lowered my head.

"But he's a hell of a sailor. One of the best I've ever known."

I smiled, my head still lowered, thinking how charming the captain could be, when he wanted to. Sure did have a silver tongue. No wonder women crooned for him.

"William, Mr. Standslong here, he wants to buy himself some moonshine. Actually, a hell of a lot of moonshine." He smiled wide, the skin crinkling along the edges of his eyes.

"Please. Call me Avalon."

"How much moonshine exactly are we talking?" I asked.

I knew it was illegal moonshine that Eli spoke about, seeing how if this Injun wanted the legal kind, he wouldn't be talking with someone like Eli. See, the captain had a tendency to teeter on the edge of shady; flirting with the law, but not quite going to bed with it.

Avalon's steely gaze swung to the captain, then hooked back on me. I suspected for sure he was contemplating the best way to scalp me. I rubbed my hair.

"Jesus, William!" Captain Cooke squawked, the laughter gone from his voice. "You don't need to bother with the details."

"I do when it's my ass on the line!"

Eli's hand reached my neck so fast that he knocked the breath out of me before I even felt the oak slam the back of my head. The playful look in his eyes had turned menacing. His lips curved in a snarl baring too white teeth for the darkness. He whispered with a controlled tongue, "You mind your manners, Mr. Lighthouse, and let me handle business details."

Pressure pushed up my neck trying to leave my ears like steam in a kettle as my pulse quickened deafeningly. Blood remained trapped in my face. Gurgling noises pressed through my lips as I tried expressing my compliance. Satisfied, Eli released his grip and I dropped to the grass sucking in mouthfuls of air. My hands rubbed my sore neck and I coughed once or twice. "Begging your pardon, sirs," I rasped on all fours.

Avalon's face was a blank canvas. The captain straightened his jacket, pushed back his hair from his eyes, and held out a hand to help me up. "Quite all right, William," he said, as if I'd tripped and fallen. "I'm sure you won't let it happen again."

"No, sir."

"Excellent." He faced Avalon. "Shall we?"

Eli motioned for the Injun to lead the way through the manicured acreage of the Governor's garden toward the front entrance. Avalon nodded, taking deliberate steps along the pebbled walkway, followed by Eli, who smiled at me over his shoulder with a wink and a nod.

As I took up the rear, I couldn't help but wonder if a lashing from Captain Cooke wouldn't be a worse experience than having my head scalped by that Injun.

PART THREE: JED TOM HUCKLEBEE

Jed Tom Hucklebee was as old as the

Appalachians themselves. A shiner since before birth, his daddy built a line of distilleries deep in the Kentucky hills. But his daddy was dead and long gone, mauled by a black bear when Jed Tom was only nine. He'd become the man of the house too fast, and the moonshine business belonged to him. No one bothered with the burden he'd been left – a sick mama and three little sisters – except a couple of farmhands and the doc, who checked in on his mama once or twice a month.

They just wanted their moonshine.

Jed Tom learned real fast that a pint of shine was worth a pair of boots, a gallon bought a horse saddle, and a whole barrel would keep his family fed with meat and grains for a month. So, he took to shining as if his life depended on it. 'Cause the truth was, it did.

Nowadays, Jed Tom was an old man of eighty-six, with two teeth left in his head full of bushy white hair. His reputation made him legendary. He didn't give a damn what poison Washington or Madison spat, what tax acts or laws they'd impose to steal money from the backwoods shiners like himself. If the people were starting a rebellion, he'd jostle up to the front lines. Ain't no way he'd let government control his family traditions.

Eli and Jed Tom sat on the front porch in wicker rockers handmade by Annabelle, Jed Tom's granddaughter. They'd been drinking moonshine since supper and were both lit pretty good. I just sat on the swing chair off to the side staying quiet. Annabelle came over offering me fresh lemonade, her soft smile and eyes in such contrast to the rough man whose blood she shared. I nodded politely and sipped my drink, the sweet and sour clashing on my tongue as I watched her hips sway gently away.

"Why'm I gonna trust some redskin? S'like trusting a coon not to steal pie cooling on the sill."

"Jed Tom, come on now," Eli said, his silver tongue reflecting the moonlight. "It's me who you'll be trusting."

"Shit. That ain't much better." He cackled a wet, raspy laugh brandished from years of too much tobacco and alcohol.

The captain smiled, navigating through his deep reserves of bullshit for the right words. "This Indian fellow is the son of a chief. He's been schooled and speaks proper English. Most times better than you."

I snickered, watching the smile turn to a scowl on the old man's face.

"That's a fact?"

Eli smirked, knocked back moonshine, then laughed out loud. "Come on, old timer." He leaned on his knees, closer to Jed Tom. "We're talking about twenty barrels here. What difference does it make if it goes to a tribe of Indians or a houseful 'a whores?'"

"Hmpff," Jed Tom snorted. "At least I'd get some at the whorehouse, yes, sir. Yes, sir. I may be old, but I ain't dead."

The two men laughed, carrying on loudly by the spirits in their cups, and I couldn't help but laugh out loud myself. Imagine that dried up old prune saddled beneath a butterball with cleavage so deep, she'd swallow up his head. Two teeth and all!

When the raucous cachinnating died, I knew what was coming and I smiled. Captain Eli Cooke was a deal closer. I'd seen him do it a hundred times, pitted against a roomful of stubborn mules, not willing to give him the time for fruition at first, ending up signing off whatever it was Eli'd sold them on, against their own better judgment.

I pitied the old man. He just didn't know.

Then, after they'd say yes, and the deal'd closed, sly old Eli would find himself a woman or two, sometimes three, and have himself a good run, finishing off the deal in his own timing. My thoughts drifted to Annabelle. Suddenly, I wasn't smiling anymore. Not her, I'd decided. I wouldn't let him.

"The fact is," Eli started, "them Injuns will be buying twenty barrels of Kentucky shine. The question is, will it be your pockets that grow fatter, or should I be taking this deal down the road?" Eli sat back, as Jed Tom shimmied forward.

"Well, well, now. Hold on, I say. I ain't said no."

Eli rocked, the planks creaking along with the wicker. He primed a cigar. Silent.

I always wondered how he was able to keep his silver tongue quiet at this point in his dealings.

"My shine's done been the best Kentucky ever made, damn straight. My pappy was a shiner, Lord knows, passing the recipe to my daddy, God rest his soul, and left to me. Three generations of the best damn shine you can find. Largest distillery around, mind you. Bet you ain't able to find no one to fill that large a order. No, sirree." He shook his head.

Eli smiled. "So, is that a yes, Mr. Hucklebee?"

Jed Tom stared at Eli as if he's a rabbit tearing up his garden. I held in my laughter, covering my mouth with my hand. "Mr. who? What's wrong with you, boy? You can call me Jed Tom like everybody else.

Shit. I ain't been called 'Mr.' since I was nine years old when my daddy died."

"Then do we have a deal, Jed Tom?" Eli asked, extending his right hand.

Jed Tom side glanced Eli, taking a deep breath. "Aw, hell," he said, grabbing hold and shaking Eli's hand firmly. "Can't have those Injuns drinking poor moonshine. And that's what you'd get going to someone else. Especially if you're needing twenty barrels, Lordy!"

Jed Tom jumped up, his knees popping, feet shuffling, hands waving, as he danced an old Irish jig.

"You've made a wise choice," Eli said.

The old man stopped midstride, peered over his hunched shoulder at the captain and said, "Don't know if I'd say that much. You're a charmer, Captain Cooke. Don't think I can't see through what you're doing here, you cocky sum'bitch."

I'd never seen the color drain from Eli's face before.

"No, sir, Captain. I'm an old man, and I know a ball buster when I see one." He smiled. "But you done made some mighty fine points, mighty fine. And I'll be damned to let you take this deal to someone else."

Eli forced his lips to curl in a smile. "Then, thank you, sir. Your honesty is a breath of fresh air."

"Ha! And your bullshit stinks!" He cackled again, kicking up his feet even higher till he was out of breath, and I watched Eli's eyes change again from playful to menacing.

The screen door opened and Annabelle stood in the doorway, her forehead wrinkled, her body stiff. "You all right, pappy?"

"I'm fine, buttercup," he snorted. "Why don't you be an angel and grab us some more to drink."

"Yes, pappy."

Jed Tom took a handkerchief from out of his back pocket and dabbed his neck and face dry. I watched Eli's gaze trailing Annabelle, and a surge of warmth flooded me. My fists clenched. "Not her," I whispered.

"She's your granddaughter, is she?" Eli remarked.

"One of 'em."

"Sure is a fine looking young woman."

"Yes, sir. Looks like her late grandmother." He stuffed the handkerchief back into his pocket. "Would you like to take a look at the 'stillery?"

"I sure would," Eli answered, standing.

"Follow me."

"William?"

I stood. "Yes, Captain," I said through gritted teeth.

"You run along with Jed Tom and get a start."

"Whatchyou gonna do?" Jed Tom asked.

"I'm gonna hang back here and wait for Annabelle to deliver our drinks." He smiled his most charming smile. "Wouldn't want her twisting her ankle in the dark on account of me."

Jed Tom nodded. "This way, boy," he motioned.

Sweat drenched and rabid, I begrudgingly followed the old man. I stole a glance over my shoulder, after Jed Tom disappeared behind the tree line, only to see Eli standing in the doorway with Annabelle – a lock of her soft hair between his fingers, a sweet smile on her lips, her laughter too quiet for me to hear – before the darkness of the forest enveloped me.

PART FOUR: BAIT AND SWITCH

"How in the hell did you convince that old timer to give you twenty barrels of moonshine with no down payment?" I asked, my eyes bulging, my mouth catching flies.

"I have my ways."

"Bet it had something to with the way you sweet talked his granddaughter," I said. The hot sun tarried on my back making me so ornery that I didn't bother holding my tongue.

Eli barely spoke over his shoulder as he navigated with the large oar. "Don't you talk about things you know nothing about."

I glared from behind as he steered us upriver, pumping my own oar into and out of the water. Sometimes, I hated Captain Eli Cooke.

The flat boat sped down the river. Green bushy trees lined the white sandy banks of the Red River. The water mirrored the blue sky spreading vast in every direction. We rounded a corner where the land pulled back in a horseshoe shape revealing a broad valley where the Caddo Village lay situated. Thirty or more large, round, log-framed houses stood like huddled women on the shore. Every inch clogged as the houses, packed tight together, formed a single impenetrable unit.

As we neared, I could see through the enlarging spaces emerging between the houses, to the grassy field in the village center. Jutting out of this field, like an arrow in a bull's eye, was a towering wooden fixture carved into a feathered snake. At the top, an image of their rain god, Chaac, stared down over his long nose; the base encircled with a perpetual ring of fire to appease their sun god.

An Injun with a long torso inked in black and green along his chest and arms stood along the riverbank awaiting our approach. I squinted in the bright sunlight.

"Is that…?"

"Avalon?" the captain said. "Yes, it is."

"I'll be damned. I wouldn't have recognized him."

"Mighty different in his top coat and hat, hmm?"

"I'll say," I muttered as our boat met the bank, the Injun's hulking figure towering over me again. He looked unruly, uncivilized, and damn right terrifying; shirtless and barefoot, his skin stretched taut over bulging muscles like red deer hide hanging out to dry.

"Welcome," Avalon said, catching the line and anchoring our Broadhorn. It was a good flat, made of solid green oak plank nearing sixty feet long, with a shed in the rear – where I presumed I'd be sleeping – and a cabin for the captain up front.

"The chief awaits."

I thought I caught Eli's eyes flinch for just a second, no longer than it takes a hummingbird's wings to flutter up and down. What for, I couldn't say. But that was the first moment I knew something wasn't right.

"Lead the way," Eli said, following Avalon up the sloping ground.

The scent of grass and damp bark filled the warm breeze. I shuffled behind, my feet kicking up the white sand of the riverbank as dust, my legs pistons running out of steam. Eli exchanged words with Avalon who nodded and continued toward the village while the captain slowed his pace till I caught up. His hands rested deep in his pockets, something the captain did when his thoughts drifted.

Something that almost always meant trouble.

"Now, William," he said, his tone caught somewhere between paternal and pleading. "I need you to do exactly as I tell you. Can you promise?"

I closed my eyes, remembering how the last time I'd made such a promise, Eli'd come running with his pants near his ankles and someone's husband shooting bullets after him.

I opened my eyes. Sweat rolled down my temples and between my shoulder blades. I was still angry with the captain for what he'd done with Annabelle, though I knew I had no right to be. I wiped my face with my sleeves. "I'll listen."

"William," he repeated. "I'm about to do something that's gonna look real bad and I need you to trust me."

I'd never seen his eyes so sincere. I crossed my arms and took a step back, hearing my own voice take on the same parental intonation. "How bad?"

"Very bad." He took a deep breath. "I'm gonna sell these here twenty barrels to the chief, but I'm not telling him that I've got them with me. I'm making him think I need to make the trade first."

My hands smacked my head. "Damn it, Captain! Have you lost your mind?"

He yanked me by my arm and swung me around beneath the covering of the surrounding woods. "No," he whispered. "I haven't lost my mind. I just need you to trust me."

"Is that how you pulled one over on the old man? Told him you had to make the trade first?"

Eli stared at me without a word. His silence was his confession.

"This is crazy, Captain. A mistake. A dastardly mistake. You're gonna get yourself killed."

He nodded. "Could."

"How are you gonna get those Injuns to give you payment for moonshine before you deliver it?"

"I'm gonna bring Avalon with me for the trade."

"What trade?" I screamed. "What trade, Captain? The damn moonshine's on the boat!" Then, I said something I probably shouldn't have, as the captain walked away from me. "You know, this ain't gonna bring her back."

The captain stopped, frozen.

I continued. "None of this law breaking, scheming, is gonna bring her—"

He charged at me, his body slamming into mine, knocking us both to the ground. He held his knife to my throat, his weight on my chest, his eyes ablaze. "Shut your mouth, William, or I swear to the Lord God Almighty I will kill you dead and let that Injun have your scalp to hang as a wall ornament. You got it?"

A tear left my eye and I tried not to piss myself.

"I'm taking my hand off you now, but you have to promise to keep quiet, keep out of my way, and do as you're told. Can you do that?"

I whimpered a stifled 'yes' through his cupped hand.

"Good." Eli rolled off my body and stood, wiping his hand off on his shirt. "Now go wait on the flat.

Stay out of the shed and Captain's quarters, and keep your eyes peeled for me and Avalon. We may need your help to carry the payment on board." He took several strides and turned back. "If you so much as blink strange to one of those Injuns, I swear I will drown you in the Red River." He kept on toward his dealing.

I trudged back to the flat boat, wiping my tears.

PART FIVE: ANNABELLE HUCKLEBEE

I baked in the sun for nearly forty minutes before I wandered under the covering of the shed. The barrels took up most of the room and it was dark except for some light slipping in through a small round window. Kerosene lamps and oil stacked in the corner. Dried meat and grains piled near the back. But something else lurked in here with me. A shadow, hiding between the barrels like a secret. I grabbed a lamp and lit it, holding my arm out to spread the light.

"Hello?" I asked. "I know you're here. Best come out...before...I shoot."

"Don't shoot."

The sweet voice, I'd know it anywhere. "Annabelle?"

She stood and I could see her beautiful face. "Don't say nothing. Please, William."

"Whatchya doing here?"

She moved out from the cramped hole she'd fit into between the moonshine. "I'm begging you. Please."

"How'd you get here? I mean, why are you here?"

"Eli brung me. He said he'd keep me safe."

Her hand brushed my forearm as ice on a burn. "From who?" I said, breaking her hold.

Her eyes lost their shimmer. "From my pappy. From his wrinkled old hands and cracked tongue."

I stared over at her, her body a leaf in the breeze. Tenderly, mimicking the way I'd heard the captain talk to women, I said, "Your pappy…he hurt you?"

She nodded. "Been sneaking into my bedroom every night since I was a little girl. Told me never to tell anyone, neither. Had his way with me, called me Eleanor. I think he believed I was my gammy."

I lowered my eyes, hate brimming in my heart. "I'm sorry, Annabelle." I jerked up. "You can't be here. You have to get off this flat."

"What? Why?"

"You just have to," I insisted, taking her by the writs and dragging her toward the door.

She pulled back, scratched me, shrieked. "I can't!"

"You have to! You gotta get back."

"I'm carrying his baby!"

Time was frost on spring blooms as I faced her, battling between pity and anger and fear. I swallowed steel nails and said, "Your pappy's?"

She shook her head.

"The captain's?" My voice inflated.

"Please. Don't make me go back home."

Voices drifted from outside the shed. I peered through the window to see the captain and Avalon several yards away, hoisting a large trunk between them. A score of redskins donned in detailed designs followed them, with their chief front and center decorated in long feathers and animal bones.

I swore. Turning to Annabelle, I said, "I won't say nothing. Not until we're back on the river."

She smiled. "Thank you, William."

I smiled quickly before rushing out the door and launching in a seat resting my feet on the railing. My arms clasped across my chest and my eyes closed. I waited for the Injuns to move closer before acting like I'd been stirred from sleep.

"We interrupting your beauty rest, Mr. Lighthouse?" the captain teased.

"No, sir," I said, jumping up to offer my assistance.

The trunk was bigger and heavier than it looked, with symbols matching the Caddo body art carved into the grainy wood. I grabbed an end as Eli boarded the flat, hefting the trunk up and over the edge while Avalon shoved from the shore. The chief's eyes glued on the trunk as if his only daughter lay buried inside. And knowing Captain Cooke, she very well could have been.

Avalon unwound the rope. Eli pushed off with the long oar. The chief took a final look at Eli and I swear his eyes faltered, the same way Eli's had when Avalon told him the chief was waiting for him; a misplaced recognition too brief for clear understanding. Taffy-like tension stretched through the air as we caught a current in the Red River pushing us closer to the mouth of the Mighty Mississip. No one spoke as the village grew smaller, and the tributary carried us onward.

Surrounded once again by green trees and white sandy banks, I said, "You wanna tell me why Annabelle Hucklebee's here?"

Avalon's head snapped up. "She's here? Where?"

"In the shed," Eli answered, his smile betrayed by the anger in his eyes. "I thought I told you to stay away from the shed."

"Maybe if you'd trusted me more, I would have been able to trust you, too."

The captain lit a pipe as Avalon skirted into the shed.

"Why didn't you tell me she was here?" I asked.

Eli blew cherry scented smoke into the air. "There's some words left unsaid till the time is right." He puffed, exhaling thick, dark smoke. "A while back, my wife went on a mission's trip into an Indian village to teach the natives what she called the four r's: reading, writing, arithmetic, and religion. She met a boy there she took kindly to, who shared the same feelings. The boy's name was Avalon Standslong."

I sat still, listening as goose pimples pressed up my skin.

"One night, these natives had a festival honoring the rain god, hoping for a bountiful harvest. They smoked heavy herbs and drank drinks so strong, they make moonshine look no worse than lemonade." Eli turned wet eyes upon me. "Those half-naked uncivilized Injuns who she came to teach and love, they raped her, William. Took turns. Then they killed my wife."

He looked away. I felt a knot in my throat. I knew all this already, except the part about the Injun, so why was he telling me? So I'd feel sorry for him and stay loyal? He'd practically raised me when I showed up on his boat nearly ten years ago when I was eleven, after I watched my papa beat my mama to death. I killed that man in our kitchen and ran. Eli Cooke took me in. Never did tell the law. Taught me to sail and fish and trade. But that didn't give him the right to treat me like shit all the time. I had opportunity staring me in the face. I was gonna be somebody, and the Governor of Virginia would be my guide from here on out. No, I wouldn't feel sorry for Captain Eli Cook anymore. He needed to get caught. Was the best thing for him.

"Avalon watched," the captain continued, "but was too young to do anything. He found my name and address, among my wife's belongings, on a letter she'd never mailed, and he kept it. When he was old enough, he left the village to continue his schooling. Found a farm where he could work for food and shelter. He worked for Jed Tom. It's where he met Annabelle.

"He found me, too. Told me the truth of what happened to my wife and told me about Annabelle, what had happened to her."

"I know," I whispered. "She told me."

Eli nodded, puffed more, and exhaled. "He also told me how much the tribe liked moonshine and about a vast treasure in their storehouse. We devised a plan to get all of them back for what they'd done. The chief, the tribe, Jed Tom, all of them. They are gonna pay for what they've done. I told you this isn't what you think it is, William. I'm not a criminal. I'm only doing what needs doing."

Avalon and Annabelle stood near me, arm in arm. I realized at that moment whose baby she carried, and that I had made a terrible mistake. A dastardly mistake. One which would most certainly cost me my life. I scanned the horizon. About a mile behind us, the large wheel of a riverboat chugged downriver.

"Captain," I said, quivering.

"What is it, William."

"You see the riverboat yonder way?"

Eli craned his neck. "Yup. What about it?"

"Well, it seems that I've made a real mess of things."

"W-i-l-l-i-a-m."

"Damn it, all," I said, running my fingers through my hair. "I thought you was just trading illegal moonshine, and nothing more. See, I'd talked with the governor in private, while you and his—" I stopped, looking over at Annabelle and feeling my ears redden. I faced the captain. "While you and Miss Carter were talking...private...."

"Yes, I get it William. When I was having sex with the governor's fiancée."

My face reddened. "Yes, sir. Then. And the governor told me he had a suspicion about you and promised me a seat in his circle, to work for Madison himself, if I turned you in." I lowered my head. "I'm sorry, Captain."

Eli jumped to his feet, staring with more interest at the riverboat. "So what you're saying, William, is that there's a riverboat coming after our flat boat."

"Yes, sir."

"And on this riverboat, there are men, maybe even the Governor of Virginia himself, fixing to arrest me for smuggling moonshine."

"That's right."

"And on this flat, we have a shitload of illegal moonshine, an Injun, a stolen treasure box, and a pregnant woman carrying a bastard child. Have I covered everything, Mr. Lighthouse?"

"Yes, sir. You have. And I suspect now you're gonna let that Injun scalp me and throw my body into the Red River for what I've done." I started to cry, like a big baby, the tears rolling down my cheeks.

"Not quite, William," Eli said.

"Really, Captain?" I stammered.

"The Injun's gonna drown you. *I'm* gonna scalp you."

"Oh, Captain!" I bawled uncontrollably.

Eli came over and took me by my shoulders. "William. I'm joking. Get a hold of yourself."

"No, Captain. You *should* kill me for what I've done. I had no idea how good you could be inside."

"It's my fault, William. I should have told you everything upfront. I'm sorry."

I looked into Eli's eyes, sniffling and whimpering, as I tried stopping my tears. His playful eyes told me everything was going to be okay. "How come you're not mad at me? You're always mad at me."

Eli placed his arm on my shoulder, the way he always had. The way a father would. "I've got nothing to be mad at anymore, William. I've made amends to my wife by saving Avalon and Annabelle, getting them to a new life in the islands where they can raise their baby, the way Clara and I always talked about."

And I understood.

"I'll make this right," I told them all. "For Clara and the baby."

PART SIX: MOONSHINE ON THE MISSISSIP'

Together, we hefted all twenty barrels of Jed

Tom's finest Kentucky moonshine into a net in the river. The riverboat was closing in less than a half mile from us.

"Grab the kerosene," I told Avalon. "Annabelle, get the lantern."

The two of them headed into the shed. I stood beside the captain watching the barrels bob in the water.

"You know what you're doing, William?" Eli asked with a smirk.

I smiled. "For the first time in my life, I believe that I do."

"Good," Eli said, taking a swig of moonshine he'd managed to salvage. "It's about damn time!"

We laughed, even in the midst of our predicament, the riverboat gaining on us, the law being broken, my dreams of entering government about to go ablaze once Avalon and Annabelle returned with what I'd asked for.

And it felt good.

It felt good to be standing beside a man as righteous as Captain Eli Cooke. My mentor, my captain, my friend. Though I'd seen him do some mighty terrible deeds, it was never at the expense of others. Even all those women he'd had relations with, they were all acting of their own accord, most probably just lonely because their husbands were too busy drinking brandy, smoking cigars, and talking politics in a dining room somewhere.

Avalon returned with five cases of kerosene. Annabelle with the lantern.

"Grab the oars, you two," I told the captain and the Injun. "Keep those barrels from edging out of the net."

I stripped off my dusty boots and socks, my bare feet skipping across the splintered deck of the ship.

"What are you gonna do?" Annabelle asked.

A sideways grin crept over my lips. "Keep you safe, ma'am."

I dove into the river.

Avalon passed me cases of kerosene and I drenched those old oak barrels till they could hold no more. The riverboat was close now and I could make out the features on Light-Horse Harry's face. And they were not pleased.

"Hand me the lantern, Annabelle, would ya?"

She leaned in, kissed me on the forehead, and smiled everything she didn't need to say. I slipped the knots holding the net to the flat boat off their nails and drifted with the barrels, the lantern held high over my head as I waded.

"Go on, now," I yelled to the captain. "Get out of here."

Eli locked eyes with mine. I'd never seen that look before. "You throw that lantern and get as far under the river as you can. We'll be waiting for you down a ways."

I nodded, knowing I never would get back on that flat boat. And I was all right with it.

Eli and Avalon pushed the oars through the water speeding away from me as fast as the riverboat approached. I could see for the very first time, and the truth was, none of it mattered, no side was correct; not the Injuns or the Union, not the shiners or the Whiskey Act. They were all capable of great evil. And the only thing that really mattered was doing the right thing whatever the cost.

I watched the flat boat grow smaller, the figures of Annabelle and Avalon and the captain disappearing from sight, while the riverboat pushed above me, hulking like a menacing creature.

And I slammed the lantern, catching the barrels and the riverboat on fire.

So, as I mentioned at the start, it was a fine spring day when Captain Eli Cooke made a terrible, dastardly mistake. But the truth was, he didn't. I was the one who made the mistake. I don't remember much after I threw that lantern, but the captain said I must have swum deep enough to get away from the flames. They found me drifting downriver a ways and pulled me on board the flat.

When I came to, we were safe on Chandeleur Island where we stayed for a few months while I recovered. We eventually worked our way to an island in the Caribbean where we stayed for many years, until Eli Cooke passed, and the Standslong's and I, after little Clara was grown up, parted ways. But it was from this adventure that I discovered who I was and who I was purposed to be. And it wasn't anything grand like being a politician or Madison's second hand man. It was bigger than that. I was destined to be the right hand man of a shady sea captain, and to help him find his peace. I was purposed to risk my life for an Indian and a molested girl carrying a bastard child to get a second chance.

Years later when I returned to Chandeleur Island, I helped erect a lighthouse on its shores; a beacon for travelers to find their way through the darkness. That was, after all, who I was. William James Lighthouse.

A man doing what needs doing.

THE END

FROM THE AUTHOR

By now, I'm sure you're wondering what in the world did I just read? I don't blame you.

The Toilet Papers came about after many of my short stories were published in small, but brilliant anthologies. I love these stories. They helped me to develop my voice, characters, and plotting before I felt courageous enough to tackle an entire novel. But no one was reading them in those books.

One day, I was thinking about my toilet book…you know, that one book that you ONLY read when you've got to go. I hate how sometimes I only need to go long enough to read a few pages or even paragraphs and then the next time I go, I can't remember where I am in the story. Or I can get a chapter or two in on some occasions (farfrompoopin'!), but still run into the problem of remembering the story.

And then, it hit me: What if there was a book separated by degrees of bowel movements? *The Toilet Papers* was born. Places to go…while you go….

A huge thank you to Linda Stay and Squatty Potty© for sharing Dookie the Unicorn's Haiku and encouraging their customers to go to places while they go by reading *The Toilet Papers*!

If you enjoyed this book, please take a moment to review it on. Thank you in advance!

Follow the author on social media @thewriteengle

Be sure to subscribe on YouTube, and if you are a fan of the stories behind legends and lore, follow the author's biweekly podcast at *ORIGINS: stories behind legends & lore* on Soundcloud and iTunes.

www.podcastORIGINS.com

Where myth and science meet.

ABOUT THE AUTHOR

Jaimie Engle: creator of cutting-edge stories with a supernatural slant, cosplayer, podcaster on ORIGINS & owner of The Write Engle, distributor of Wick Books[tm], the story-scented candle line for JME Books.

When she isn't making up stories, she's probably drinking coffee somewhere, playing trivia, or teaching about writing. Become a fan at thewriteengle.com.